Copyright © 2018 by Lovestruck Romance Publishing, LLC.

All Rights Reserved.
No part of this publication may be reproduced, distributed or transmitted in any form or by any means including photocopying, recording, or other electronic or mechanical methods except in the case of brief quotations embodied in critical reviews and certain other noncommercial uses permitted by copyright law. The unauthorized reproduction or distribution of this copyrighted work is illegal.

This book is a work of fiction. Names, characters, businesses, places, events, and incidents are either the products of the author's imagination or used in a fictitious manner. Any resemblance to actual persons living or dead is purely coincidental.

This book is intended for adult readers only.
Any sexual activity portrayed in these pages occurs between consenting adults over the age of 18 who are not related by blood.

FIRE BREATHING BEAST

DRAGONS OF THE BAYOU

CANDACE AYERS

LOVESTRUCK ROMANCE PUBLISHING, LLC

Sky Broussard has spent the last nine years of her life fighting for custody and then raising her now teenage nephews. Between trying to make ends meet as a waitress at the Bon Temps Café, and keeping an eye on two troublesome teens, she's had zero time for indulging in things like romance.

No worries, she hasn't been interested in the opposite sex for a long time. Until, she meets the snarling, growling, hotter-that-an-inferno guy who caught her nephews trespassing on his property deep in the Louisiana bayou.

Too bad he's off his rocker. Seriously. He thinks he's a dragon, calls her his mate, follows her home, and refuses to leave her side. She really should put a stop to the insanity. She really should. Except, her libido is running on overdrive and he might be her chance to finally lose her V-card.

1
SKY

I had a table of six teenagers who thought it was funny to shoot soda out their straws across the table at one another. *Beautiful.* A nasty, sticky mess and—I'd stake my life on it—a crap tip. Not only that, but I'd probably be waiting on them for another hour while they horsed around making messes until a parent of one of them came to pick them up. They were around the same ages as my nephews, and wildly immature.

Not that Casey and Nick were all that mature. They weren't. They just had a different type of immaturity. I glanced to the rear of the café. The boys were in the back office doing their homework, their typical routine after school when I was working a shift. It was a Monday night and the teachers at the charter school they attended had loaded them down with work. Still, they needed to be checked on every so often to make sure they were behaving. Otherwise, one never knew what those boys might get into. What was that saying about idle hands?

I spotted Nick's size thirteen tennis shoes poking out of the office doorway and I couldn't stifle the sigh that escaped my lungs at the sight. The kid wouldn't stop growing. He was already a half a foot taller than me and at six foot, it didn't look like he was slowing down anytime soon. His feet weren't slowing down, either. That pair of tennis shoes protruding past the doorjamb were the fourth pair I'd bought him in the last twelve months.

"I can't believe Kayla is really going to ask Danny to the dance." A high-pitched voice rang out across the crowded café. "Ugh, how embarrassing for her. Danny already told me he likes me and he thinks she's an ugly cow."

I looked back at the table. Danny's apparent love interest was a pretty blonde with a nasty snarl and an upturned nose. While the rest of the table laughed, my heart went out to poor Kayla.

"She *is* a cow. I don't know why you still hang out with her."

"Do you see her here?"

More laughter. I blew out a long breath. I was starting to think that I was too old for this, but I wasn't. It was the mileage not the years.

"Sky, can you drop this at table four? I need to run to the back and check my phone." Amie, the other waitress, held a tray of food out to me and flicked her eyes to the back. "I'm waiting to see about the test results."

I took it from her and smiled. "Of course. I'm crossing my fingers for you."

She was trying to get pregnant. Having custody of two teens, I sometimes wondered *why* she wanted it so badly, but I was hopeful for her. In my mind, a woman went through the pain of childbirth only to end up eventually with teenagers who considered you the bane of their existence. At least I was able to have avoided the "pain of childbirth" part and gone right to the "evil lord overseer" part. Casey and Nick were my brother's kids, not my own, as they liked to remind me.

I dropped the food off at table four, got them a fresh bottle of ketchup and glanced again at the back. Marcus, the owner, didn't mind the kids being around after school, but I didn't want to wear out our welcome. I had nowhere else to send them.

Nick's shoes were still there, but at an odd angle. Humph. A *really* odd angle. My stomach dropped. I hurried back to see what was up and found Amie sitting alone at Marcus' desk. Nick's shoes had been propped up using the bottles from the cokes I'd grabbed for him and Casey earlier. Crap! I knew I wouldn't find them in the kitchen, but I looked anyway. No luck. A door led out to the back alley. I already knew they were gone.

"It was negative." Amie's voice cracked and broke through my anger. "I'm not pregnant."

"Oh, Amie, I'm so sorry."

She shook her head and climbed to her feet. "It's like the good book says, right? To everything there's a season." She blew out a rough breath.

I wrapped her in a quick hug, a comfort-squeeze, then gestured towards Nick's shoes. "I know of a couple of kids for sale or rent. You can get 'em super cheap today. Bargain basement prices."

"No, thanks." She edged Nick's shoes out of the way and then pushed her shoulders back and jutted out her chin. "It'll happen when it happens."

"That's right, chère. Keep your spirits up." I tried to comfort Aime, but my anxiety sky rocketed as I scanned the café. It was packed and from what I could tell, a few of my tables needed tending to. Looked like table six could use drink refills, eleven was nearing either dessert or their check, and table eight should be just about ready to order. Shoot. I couldn't just go after the boys. Marcus was an understanding boss, for the most part, but skipping out during the dinner rush was not a forgivable offense at the Bon Temps Café. If I attempted to slide out and look for them, he'd have my hide, not that I could blame him.

My stomach knotted in worry. Those boys. I couldn't afford to lose my job. I'd have to pray now and search for their butts later. Hopefully, they wouldn't get themselves into too big 'a trouble while I finished out my shift.

I did what any good worker in a service job does and swallowed my personal issues while plastering a phony smile on my face. In my head, though, I was raging. I took a few deep breaths and tried to extinguish the imaginary shouting match I was having with Nick in my head. He was the older of the two and at sixteen, he knew better.

As much as I wanted to yell and scream at him to stop dragging Casey into troublesome predicaments and start stepping up and helping out, a huge part of me just felt sorry for him. Sure, he put me through some major stress, but they'd both weathered pretty tough storms in their young lives.

I got that they were angry and lost but, lord ha' mercy, Casey had just turned fourteen and he'd already been picked up by the police twice. Each time, somehow, Nick had mysteriously been absent. But, I wasn't born yesterday. I suspected Nick had been close by and probably the orchestrater of the goings on—at least close enough to have had his hand in the cookie jar, so to speak. Nick had managed to be picked up a few times, too. Maybe he'd just gotten wiser at staying out of reach of the long arm of the law, but it wasn't like Casey to get into trouble all by himself.

They'd run away from the café before. They hated sitting in the back and waiting on me, but I couldn't allow them to stay in the house by themselves. It wasn't safe for mischievous teenage boys to be left alone unsupervised. Of course, it wasn't fair of me to take up a table in the front when the place was swamped with paying customers, either. That was no way to keep a job I desperately needed.

I realized I was going around in circles in my head, frustrated and scared. Stepping in and taking over the raising of teenage boys when I had only just learned how to care for myself was so darn hard and I really sucked at it. But, I'd be damned straight to the fiery infernos of H-E-double toothpicks if I'd let those boys go off to be separated and raised by strangers. Not in my lifetime.

I hated it when they ran off. They didn't have phones—it wasn't in our budget—and I never knew where they were. Part of me, somewhere in the back of my mind, was just waiting on a call that would turn everything upside down and change it forever. Again.

"Look alive, chère. Your table of toddlers are ready to split without paying."

I snapped to attention and hurried over to them. "Oh, y'all weren't trying to slip away before you settled the bill, were you?"

A boy who looked similar to Nick in height and build shook his head. "Er, no, ma'am."

"Oh, thank heaven 'cause you see the owner, Marcus…he's a little cuckoo for cocoa puffs if y'all know what I mean. And nothing gets his goat more than patrons who dine and dash. I'll let you in on a little secret. He keeps a sawed-off shotgun behind the counter for just such occasions. You know, when people try to leave without paying for the food that he purchases, Big Jay cooks, I serve and clean up after. His finger's been *real* slippery lately, too."

The nasty, snarling blonde girl elbowed the tall boy and whispered to him. "Just pay her."

"*You* pay her. You're the one who wanted to come here!"

I put my hands on my hips and cocked my head to the side. "I don't care who pays, as long as one of y'all does before Marcus and his twitchy finger go for the sawed-off. I am so not in the mood to clean up blood tonight. Last time I ruined a perfectly good pair of jeans."

A twenty was quickly thrust into my hand and the lot of them fled the restaurant like they'd just seen Freddy Krueger. I grabbed their bill and swore under my breath. A twenty cent tip. La-di-da. Little shits.

Amie came up beside me, balancing her tray on her hip. "What'd they tip you? Fifty cents?"

"Twenty."

She groaned. "We should chase them down and talk to their parents."

"We should chase them down and beat 'em up for their lunch money."

"You both should get back to work and stop fantasizing about robbing our young patrons." Marcus lightly squeezed both of our shoulders and then nudged us away.

I spared one last glance back at the empty office and blew out a breath. *Please, Lord, let them be okay.*

2

BEAST

Seventy-five years and I still missed the old world. The swamps of southern Louisiana's delta basin were fine, but they weren't the same. I'd done my best to build my castle in this human world, but something about the place wasn't home. I missed the massive towering castles where I used to perch as a youngling on the centuries old stone turrets and breathe fire at anyone who dared approach.

I listened to the two males creep closer. Still about a mile out, I heard them as they crossed over my property line. I couldn't suppress the grin. Fortunately, I still got to have a bit of fun once in a while. By the way they were navigating the marsh, they were traveling with a purpose. It wasn't the first time humans had come nosing around to see what was lurking deep in the interior of the swampland, although, due to the stories and rumors, it was a rare occurrence.

Some said, usually in whispers, that a voodoo priestess had cursed the area and all who ventured far enough into the swamps were damned. Others spoke of the rougarou, Cajun werewolves, frequenting the area. Luckily, superstitions were rampant in this part of the deep south and tales of sinister happenings deep in the bayou were handed down from mothers to babes. Once a body entered, they said, he might never return.

The stories and rumors were all started by yours truly, of course. I wasn't a fan of trespassers. Besides, if they knew the *real* truth, they'd run for their weak, puny, little lives. The way my enemies of old once had.

My nostalgic reminiscing of the old world was expressed in a long, low sigh and I sank into the cushioned chair that the human interior designer had sworn I would love. Surprisingly, I did. That was one thing the old world didn't have, these chairs. What had the squeaky human male called it? Ah, yes, an ergonomic exterior patio lounger and recliner. Strange name for a chair. I kicked my feet up on the stool that accompanied it and gazed out at my swamp. A napping alligator lounged nearby, not a care in the world. He liked to remain close when I was outdoors and I figured he was better to have around than one of those yapping little furry creatures that humans seemed to love.

I breathed in the thick air. It was warm and heavy and caused my clothes to cling to my body and beads of sweat to pearl across my forehead. *That,* at least, was a familiar feeling. The heat in the new world wasn't all that different than the heat from fire breathing.

The two human males were getting closer. They were both quiet, probably assuming they were approaching undetected. The smile of joyous anticipation that spread across my face arose from my deepest internal depths, a smile from the beast that I harbored—the beast that I *was*. The males had no clue what manner of terror they were about to encounter.

Suddenly, Cezar's annoying voice sounded in my head reminding me that we didn't eat humans. *Fuck.* I kicked the stool away angrily. What fun was life without being able to flame and devour those who thought they could sneak up and catch you off-guard?

Cezar and, well, *all* the dragons had adjusted to this place better than I had. They weren't like me. They were babied, coddled, little fire breathing lumps. They'd learned and followed human rules and customs and didn't seem to mind that we'd had to flee our own world, that we were forced to *chill* here, as Blaise always put it. I minded. I'd owned and presided over a vast territory in the old world. I'd ruled with such great power and might that—

My thoughts were interrupted. The males, mere younglings from the scent, were edging closer still. I'd have plenty of time to finish my mental rant later. Right then, I had trespassers that needed to be dealt with.

As if sensing the overwhelming predatory response in me, the alligator swung his tail and snapped his teeth before sliding effortlessly back into the water.

I stood from my chair. Too bad. It was so comfortable I hated to leave it. Another reality of the human world. It encouraged laziness.

I slipped into the swamp behind the alligator and positioned myself so I could see the young males when they got closer. They'd been wordless up until that point. For some reason, they waited until they were almost right on top of my home to break their silence. Hunters, they were not.

"Sky is going to kill us, Casey."

"No, she won't. She'll have a shit fit and then she'll get over it, like she always does. She won't stay mad forever. She'll cool off eventually."

"One of these days, she *is* going to stay mad. And then what? What do we do then?"

"Then, we figure something else out."

"Something else?" The older male raised his voice. "You're an idiot, you know that? There *is* no something else. She's it. She's all we got."

"Just shut up. We're almost there. Josh said that this is it, right up here, around the last bend."

"What's the point of this, anyway?"

"To see the swamp monster, duh."

"This is why I shouldn't let you talk me into things. You sneak out and get us into trouble doing stupid childish shit like trying to see a monster in a swamp. Does it look anything like the Creature from the Black Lagoon? How old are you, anyway? Fourteen going on five?"

"Oh, eat shit."

"*You* eat shit."

They were right in front of me at that point. I stepped silently in front of their boat, shielded by the cover of nightfall and dense vegetation. "You both can eat shit."

Both boys screamed as I lifted the boat out of the water like it weighed nothing. Then, I turned it over and dumped them out of the boat and into the dark, murky water. When they came up, they were still screaming. I tossed their boat towards the dock before picking them both up by the backs of their necks.

"Just what the fuck are you doing in my swamp?"

"Don't kill us! We just wanted to come and see the swamp mon—uh—" The smaller male smelled like fear and urine, so I dunked him back into the water.

"We're sorry, m-mister. We're sooo sorry. We'll go. We'll go right now and we won't tell a soul! Not one single, solitary soul." The bigger one was frightened, but he also scented of determination. He was the protector, although, from the sound of it, he'd allowed the smaller one to lure him into trouble.

"Why did you come to my swamp?"

The little one shivered. "My friend said that he saw a...a swamp monster."

I grinned, knowing my smile could in no way be interpreted as light and friendly. "You want to see a monster? You've come to the right place. I'll show you a monster."

They both shook their heads, or tried to. With me holding their necks, the movement looked more like a spasm. The small one's eyes filled with tears. "No, please. Let us go. Don't kill us. Our Aunt Sky will come looking for us!"

"And what do you think your *Aunt Sky* is going to find when she comes looking for you? Nothing but your bare bones picked clean after I've roasted you over an open flame, slathered with my favorite Cajun hot sauce. I'll devour every tender morsel of your flesh."

They both started struggling harder to get away, but their efforts were in vain. They were helpless against my superior strength. When they tired themselves sufficiently, I dropped them back into the water. Then, I pondered what to do with them. Cezar's voice filtered into my head again, demanding I send them home to their adult.

"No! They are intruders and must be dealt with. I shall—"

"They're babies."

"Hah! The ruffians have broached my territory."

"Let. Them. Go. Release them to their adult."

He annoyed me sometimes. Nevertheless, I grabbed their shirtfronts and dragged them through the water. "Come on. We must summon your adult to come and retrieve you."

"We can just take our boat back home, sir."

I pulled them faster. "No. We must call." Damn Cezar.

"It's late. If we call our Aunt Sky, she's going to be majorly pissed at us. And, we took her boat while she was at work. She won't even be able to get here."

"Too bad."

I dragged them to my house where I dug around in a kitchen drawer until I found the phone that Cezar had demanded I take. I tossed it to the older male and nodded at it. "Call."

"But—"

I grabbed the little one and sniffed him. "I think I'll start with his arms."

"Fine!" He screamed. "I'm calling! I'm calling!"

3

SKY

I jerked upright when my phone rang. I'd fallen asleep at the kitchen table while worrying and waiting for the boys to come home. I grabbed my phone and snapped it open.

"Nick? Casey?"

Nick's voice was quiet as it came over the line. "Um…Aunt Sky?"

I stood up and clutched at my chest. "What is it? What's wrong? Are you at the police station? The emergency room? Oh god, where's Casey? Is he with you? Please tell me he's with you."

There was more hesitation. "We're okay. I think."

"Where are you, Nick?" I was already grabbing the keys to my beat up Ford pickup. "Just tell me where you are and we'll figure the rest out later."

"We're out on the swamp. Past Bulcon Bay."

I stopped and dropped my car keys. "Nick, you took the boat? How am I supposed to get to you?"

"I don't know, Sky, but please come and get us before this guy eats us!"

"Where past Bulcon Bay? How far?"

"I…I don't know." He spoke to someone in the background and then muttered out more directions.

I got the idea, at least enough to find the general area. I'd been raised in the bayou and knew parts of it like the back of my hand. I could navigate the swamps well enough to get me close to the place Nick described. Along with my familiarity of the swampland came an awareness and respect for it that the boys obviously didn't possess. It was idiotic to tempt mother nature by venturing deep into the bayou at night. The swamps weren't safe. They were chock full of gators and other creatures waiting under the surface of the water to strike out at whoever was stupid enough to disrespect its inherent danger.

Me, apparently. At that moment, I was stupid enough. "I'll be there as soon as I can."

The clock on the wall was not my friend and I swore when I realized that it was almost midnight. No one would be awake to loan me a boat. My neighbor, Jude, would be pissed at me, but I'd just have to take his and apologize later. Extreme situations called for extreme measures and all that, and this was an emergency.

I raced out of the house, the screen door flapping closed behind me, and crept back behind Jude's house. His boat was moored to the little dock in his back yard, welcoming me. I knew he kept the key in the shed by his back porch, so I crept over and opened the door as quietly as I could, feeling around for the hook. I snatched the key and took off running out to the boat just as I heard Jude's back door open.

"What the hell are you doing?!" The angry voice of my nearest neighbor bellowed through the night.

"I'm sorry, Jude! It's an emergency. I have to go get the boys. They've got my boat and they're in trouble!" I untied it and started the motor almost in one fluid motion and gunned it away from the dock.

"When are they *not* in trouble? Come on, Sky. This is theft."

"I'm bringing it back, Jude. That's not theft; it's borrowing. I'll make it up to you, I swear."

He stood with his hands on his hips, glaring at me—a look so fuming I could see it in the pale light cast by the sliver of a moon. I debated offering a friendly wave as I turned a corner on the little waterway behind our houses, venturing farther into the swamp. Naw, that would only piss him off. An apology and a plate of freshly baked chocolate chip cookies would probably be a better way to restore our neighborly harmony. I'd worry about it tomorrow.

I switched on the spotlight at the front of Jude's boat and shivered as the illumination immediately caught the eyes of a big gator. The night was as thick, hot, and as damp as I'd ever felt it and I navigated the tall grass, cattails, and murky water with the skill of someone who'd been doing it all her life. My worn T-shirt quickly soaked through and stuck to my body. The song of chirping crickets and croaking bullfrogs was accompanied by occasional howls and grunts, the night melody of the bayou. It would have been peaceful if not for the deadly predators that awaited those foolish enough to be out at after dark.

The swamp was beautiful at times, with its thick cypress trees and hanging moss, it's lush presence that took you back to another time. No matter how many Walmarts and Applebees sprung up in other parts of the world, out in the bayou, you felt like you'd been transported back to prehistoric times.

My daddy had been lost in a swamp not far from the one I was navigating. A drunk and a hapless fool, he'd gone out in a drunken stupor to kill a gator. In his brilliant, inebriated state, he'd decided that a pair of gator skin boots would bring him the good luck that always seemed just beyond his grasp. His boat had been found a few days later, nothing in it but some crushed beer cans and enough blood to convince the sheriff, and everyone else, that he'd been the meal of the very gator he'd been trying to turn into footwear. How's that for luck?

I shivered again as I steered the boat around a fallen log. Creepy-ass nighttime swamp. The more I thought about the boys being out there, the angrier I got. Maybe I needed to be stricter with them. That might curb these crazy stunts they pulled. Maybe I was too strict. Maybe they felt that the reins I held on them were too tight and they were rebelling. It's not like there was a guidebook on how to raise boys for an aunt who was barely old enough to be their mother but fought tooth and nail to pull them out of the foster care system and give them a permanent home. Regardless, if they were alive and well, I was going to kill them.

From the snippets of information I'd gotten on the phone, I gathered they'd run into someone who didn't like whatever they'd been doing. Nick had sounded blatantly scared. There was no telling who they'd run into that deep out. I knew the rumors. I'd heard the superstitious tales of rougarou and curses of voodoo queens. I didn't believe one lick of any of those crazy superstitions, but that didn't mean that I didn't think there was something dangerous out in those parts. Although, my guess was it was probably something human. Like backwoods folk who preferred to stay secluded and keep to themselves. People best left alone. Maybe they were even inbred, or like those guys in the movie, *Deliverance*. Yeah, that was my guess.

My worry made it feel like a lifetime to get past Bulcon Bay and then another lifetime to continue on as far as Nick had told me to go. Rustling of leaves and branches overhead in the canopy of trees jangled my already thinly stretched nerves. Then there was the worst—the abrupt plunk and splash. Something that was nearby, something unseen, had just entered the water. Probably a gator. Maybe a turtle or a snake, but probably a gator.

I'd never been this far. No one came out this far. A turn through an arch made by the root system of a very old, very dead tree marked my last leg of the trip.

The light on Jude's boat cut a path through a narrow channel, surrounded on both sides by looming cypresses. Massive roots jutted out, mute warnings of what peril lay ahead. Then, abruptly, the path opened to the mouth of a small lake.

Up ahead through the mist, I could just make out a large silhouette taking up the night sky like some sort of—was that a castle? The closer I got to the immense structure, the more I was half certain it *was* a castle. Some sort of modern castle, with sleek stone walls and lots of glass that didn't offer a view of the inside of the place. Okay, so maybe these weren't backwoods inbred folk.

My boat was there, tied to a small dock at the head of the expanse of swamp. I steered up next to it and tied Jude's boat next to mine then climbed onto the dock. A stone path led to what looked like a patio. A castle with a patio? For some reason, maybe my jangled nerves, that seemed funny to me and I let out a little snort.

My humor was short lived. On the patio, an ottoman was knocked over on its side, reminding me of how scared Nick had sounded. Whoever had them might even have roughed them up for trespassing. I pounded on the large metal door. Hard. Well, it was huge and the size, along with the fact that it was made of galvanized steel, seemed to warrant a hard pounding. Plus, my boys were in there somewhere, possibly hurt, certainly scared. I knocked harder. My knuckles ached, but I kept knocking.

Finally, the door opened and on the other side loomed the largest, most muscular, well-built, handsomest man I'd ever seen. Oh, lordy, he was not inbred. Not at all. No, siree, not at all. In some freakish turn of events, my body reacted to him, heating instantly, and I practically drooled as I gaped at him. Every delicious inch of him.

I forced myself to pull it together. I had no excuse for wasting time gawking at the sexy stranger. The man had my nephews somewhere in the place. I pushed past him. The light brush of my bare forearm against his sucked the breath right out of my body. Shivers. Delicious shivers. What the holy hell was wrong with me?

"Nick! Casey!" My voice shook, quivering with emotion. I bit my lip and looked around. The immense house felt even larger on the inside because of all the open space. The ceilings were at least three stories high. More smooth stone and modern design. The windows were one-way glass and offered what must have been, in the daylight, an amazing view of the surrounding wetland.

"Little human. Come here." His voice was a deep growl that I felt in a tingle from the top of my head all the way to my toes. It also stopped everywhere in between.

I looked back at him, despite my better judgement. He was still at the door, his big body blocking the exit, his eyes burning into me. Had he just referred to me as a little *human*? "Where are they?"

"You smell amazing." As if to prove his point, he tipped his head back slightly and took a deep inhale.

I stepped back. *What the...?* My insides were still doing cartwheels, but my brain was working out something—something niggling just out of its reach. Something was weird about the hottie. I nodded at him, trying to placate him so I could find my nephews and get the hell out of there.

"Come here." He put his hands on his hips and stood there, apparently expecting me to obey him.

"Um...*no*."

He growled. "Mate, *come here*."

Nick and Casey picked that exact moment to run into the big open area. They didn't look too scared, though. They looked excited and—mesmerized. "Aunt Sky! Isn't this place awesome?"

I was really going to kill them.

4
BEAST

I was going to bite the heads off the little human males. What the fuck were they doing, interrupting my first meeting with my mate? My *human* mate. That was entirely unexpected. She was little, *so* little. How would she be sexually compatible with a man as large as me?

The younger male, who I'd learned was called Casey, had gotten over his fear. He was awed by me. He spoke non-stop—dragon this and dragon that—naturally impressed. Maybe I should've hidden my nature from him, refrained from disclosing the truth, but I wasn't ashamed of it. I was proud of my strength and great stature, both as a man and as a dragon. I wouldn't hide it.

"Come on, boys. We're going home." My little mate reached for the young males, but they slipped away from her.

The smaller male was argumentative. "No. Come on. You're already here. Look around. It's so cool."

Her pale skin flushed red and I scented her frustration. It came off of her in waves tainting the delectable scent I'd previously detected—the faint aroma of arousal. I was again tempted to eat the smaller male.

"Casey. You snuck off, stole the boat, got stuck out here, and called me to come get you in the middle of the night. I don't want to look around. I want to get you boys home and get us all to bed. I work in the morning."

"You don't even get it." He crossed his arms and scowled at her. "You *would* ruin it. You suck."

Before I even gave it a split second's thought, I was across the room growling an ominous warning in the small male's face. "You do *not* speak to my mate like that."

He paled, but just sighed and shrugged. "Fine. Can we come back, though?"

The older boy, Nick, was still on guard, more apprehensive of me. He looked from me to Casey and shook his head. "Come on, Casey. Listen to Aunt Sky. We have to go."

My mate was giving me a strange look. I didn't care how she looked at me as long as she remained there, in my home. She smelled like heaven, reminding me of the sweet scent of the tiny blossoms that bloomed only once every hundred years in the old world, and only after a rain shower. Her beckoning lips were turned down in a frown and I found myself yearning to touch them. She was plump and soft in all the right places and I could already feel myself hardening, readying to mount her. I drank her in with my eyes, studying her delectable curves from inch to inch.

A step closer to her, and I was certain I smelled the beginnings of her arousal once again. Her nostrils flared and the stunning pale brown of her eyes was eaten up by the widening of her pupils.

"You will stay, mate."

That strange look returned and she took a step away from me. "Why do you keep calling me that? We're not friends. Are you Australian? I just came to get the kids. Now, we're outta here."

I growled from deep in my chest, startling all of them. The sound was low and rough, an audible claiming of this human female in front of me. I wanted my mate. I needed her. I longed to sink my teeth into the soft flesh of her shoulder, to couple with her and pleasure her for hours. I wanted to taste the blood that rushed through her veins so hard that I could practically see it thrumming under her skin. The bloodlust that arose when a dragon found his mate was something evolutionary that I'd never understood fully before. I wanted to taste her blood because it would mean that I'd pierced through her delicate skin and marked her as my own. That taste meant forever.

My mate took another few steps back dragging with her another growl from deep in my body. She couldn't get away from me. She was mine.

"Boys, get outside. Now."

Nick tugged Casey, but the smaller male was digging in his heels, showing a stubborn streak that I would have appreciated, if he hadn't been directly disobeying my mate's command. "Come on, Sky. I want to stay and look around more."

"Do as she says."

"Don't yell at them!" My mate grabbed Casey's arm and pulled him towards the door. "Go wait outside, Casey. I'm not kidding. Get in that boat and wait on me, or you're going to be grounded for the rest of your life."

"You can't ground me. I don't have to listen to you. You're not my mother."

"Casey! Go!" Pain, anger and frustration created a sour scent from her and when she looked back at me, her eyes were shiny with moisture.

I closed the gap between us and slid my hand to the back of her head, tilting it and staring down at her. I traced my finger under her eye. Wetness. Tears. A stabbing pain like I'd never experienced before shot through my chest. She was *crying*. Not only was she crying, but it was tearing my heart out.

"What are you doing?" Her voice was quiet, but rushed, as she stared up at me with wide eyes.

"He made you cry. I shall kill him."

Her eyes widened and she jerked away. "That's enough crazy talk, Mr. Looneytunes. We're going. I'm sorry they bothered you. I can assure you that they will get a long, stern talking to about trespassing."

"You can't leave. You're my mate. You must stay."

"Excuse me?" She shook her head and pushed the boys towards the door. "We're going home."

"Then I will come with you." I shrugged. If she didn't like my home, I would just go to hers. Maybe my little castle was not as nice as her dwelling. I didn't know why she seemed against it, but we'd work it out.

"Um...no, you're not." Nick opened the door and she practically dragged Casey out towards the dock.

I breathed in a lungful of the hot, muggy night air and nodded to the alligator who was back in his usual spot. He whipped his head around at the three humans and hissed.

My mate screamed and shooed the boys behind her, shielding them with her body. That wouldn't do. I stepped past the boys and wrapped my arm around her waist to pull her behind me. Staring down at the alligator, I let out my own hiss, coupled with a flash of fire.

It was enough of a warning to scare him away. He snapped his big jaws and slunk back into the water.

The threat to my mate handled, I focused in on the sensation of my arm around the softness of her waist. Soft and warm, I wanted to bury my face in her curves and inhale her scent until I was full of her and dizzy with the desire to mate her.

She let me hold her, her full chest heaving as she gripped my arm. Once her fear subsided, though, she spun to face the boys. "This is why I don't want you doing stuff like this. You could've been killed! You go out into the swamp in the middle of the night and you take chances with your lives! It's dangerous out here!"

I was still holding her, having turned with her, and could feel her shivering against me. I flattened my hand against her stomach and pulled her flush against my body. "Remain calm, little one."

She spun back around to face me, her full breasts pressing right up against me like soft, sensual pillows. I couldn't take my eyes off of them. "They could've been killed! There are any number of dangers out here in the daytime, not to mention at night when visibility is nil and predators come out to hunt. But for divine grace they escaped getting really hurt."

"*I* kind of wanted to really hurt the small male for making you cry."

"That alligator was too close..." She was crying again. Big, wet tears that ran down her cheeks and landed on her shirt.

Nick came to his senses first. He laid his hand on her shoulder and looked up at me, then his aunt. "We're sorry, Sky. We messed up."

Even the smaller one, who I was still considering eating, or at least scaring harshly, seemed to sober at the sight of her tears. "Yeah, sorry."

I rubbed her back, the instinct to provide comfort and protection was shocking to me, but gladly accepted. I was not known for my softness nor did I possess a particularly tender nature. I'd never comforted anyone before. I was a dragon, for fire's sake. "Come back inside. I will offer you a glass of whiskey. It will make you feel better."

She instantly pulled away from me and shook her head looking puzzled. "This is crazy."

5
SKY

What the hell was I doing letting the giant, hunky hulk of a man hold me, touch me, and tenderly stroke my back? He acted like he knew me somehow. And, why wasn't I reacting the way I should've been, which was to say *in horror*. He kept telling me he was going to keep me in his house and that I was his mate. He was clearly disturbed, maybe even Jeffrey Dahmer disturbed. Yet, the man turned me on like a light switch. Nothing and no one else had ever gotten me all hot and bothered before the way he was doing with his gentle caresses. Goodness, this was new, unexpected, and not entirely welcome on my part. I'd never even had a serious relationship with a man before. Ever.

His arms around me ignited a fire in my belly that threatened to burn straight through my clothing. I ached to get closer to him.

He was certifiable, though. Obviously. He'd threatened to kill Casey, faced off with a gator like it was a gnat, and he *growled*. Even if the growling did strangely turn me on, it was still weird. Wasn't it?

When I finally forced myself to pull away from him, it was not easy. It felt like there was an elastic cord tugging me back to him. I had to fight the urge to sink back into his chest. "We have to go."

"To your castle?"

I snorted without meaning to. "Yeah, my castle. Sure." Turning to the boys, I motioned for them to head to Jude's boat. "Get in."

Nick pulled a mopey and sour-faced Casey with him into the mud boat and they both sat at the front, giving me room to sit at the back and control the rudder. As I raised my foot to step inside, the man put his hand on my arm.

"I'm coming with you."

I shook my head. "No, you're not. You're staying here, with your pet alligator, in your big house that is oddly displaced in the middle of the bayou."

He stepped easily into the boat ahead of me and settled into the back where I needed to be to steer the boat out of the swamp. "Get in."

"You can't go with us. I mean it. You live here. You need to step out of the boat and go on back into your house. Castle. Whatever."

"I'm coming." He shook his head. "Are you always so argumentative?"

Casey laughed. "Yes."

The man growled at him again. "I'm still imagining ways to skin you for your treatment of my mate. Don't push it, small male."

That shut Casey up. It lit a fire under me, though. "Don't you talk to him like that. You keep threatening my boys and I'm going to call the cops on you."

"The *cops*? Really?" He seemed amused, then frustrated. Then, he narrowed his eyes. "Are you friendly with one of them? Does he give you gifts? Shower you with attention?"

Give me gifts? "Are you asking if I'm dating a cop?"

"Are you?"

"No."

"Good." Then, he stood up and grabbed me. Easily lifting me into the boat, he settled me on his lap and wrapped an arm around my waist. Sheesh, it felt like a steel bar. "Hold on. Not you, Casey. It would do you good to get a dunking."

I pulled and pushed at his arm wiggling and trying to get away, but my efforts were in vain. "You can't do this. You can't just—"

The boat started and we shot forward. He hadn't even turned the boat light on. It was pitch black the farther away from his house we got. "I can and I am."

I fought harder. We were in total darkness. The light from the sliver of crescent moon was unable to poke through the thick canopy of trees and moss and he was going way too fast. "Stop! Turn the lights on! You're going to kill us all!"

He grumbled and leaned closer, his mouth right next to my ear. "I can see perfectly fine. And while I am still making up my mind about the young male, I would never kill you. You are my mate. I will protect you with my very life. I will care for you and pleasure you and tend to your every desire."

At his mention of pleasure and desires, I felt his rock-hard erection poking me. Whoa, it was big. I hadn't realized what it was at first because of the sheer size of it. Gasping and looking back at him, I found that I couldn't see his face, it was so dark. Being submerged in total darkness, held practically immobile by a stranger, should've felt oppressively frightening. Yet, sitting on his lap feeling how excited he was wasn't frightening at all. It was the hottest I'd ever been. I could feel moisture leaking out of my core, my crazy, usually non-existent, libido was all of a sudden shooting off like fire crackers.

"Little one, I can smell how much you want me, too."

I jerked upright and faced forward, instantly mortified. He was a stranger. A stark raving mad stranger who was holding me against my will and carting me off to who knew where.

"Where's your home?"

Okay, he was carting me off to my home, but still. He was obviously out of his mind. And how was it he could he see to navigate?

"Boys, are you okay?"

They both muttered an affirmative answer, at least letting me relax slightly about that for the time being.

I lowered my voice and spoke over my shoulder to the stranger. "Why are you doing this?"

His hand flattened against my stomach again and his thumb

stroked just under my breast. "You're mine. Do you not feel our connection?"

His. I told myself to be angry and to free myself from his grip, because that's what a normal woman would do. But, there was something about the weirdo saying those words that sent my heart racing and fire burning through my veins. What was wrong with me?

I told him where we lived and settled against his chest as he navigated the boat smoothly. "Who are you?"

"Beast."

"What?"

"Beast." He repeated himself a little louder like I might be hard of hearing.

"*Beast*?" I said it like it was acid on my tongue. "That's your name?"

"Yes. And you're Sky."

"What kind of name is Beast?"

"It's a dragon's name, *Sky*," Casey called from the front of the boat. "He's a dragon."

I sighed. "Of course. He's a dragon. This just gets better and better."

Beast chuckled from behind me. Then, his mouth pressed against the side of my neck and his breath flitted down my neck and under the collar of my shirt. "A dragon, little one. A big, fire-breathing dragon who wants nothing more than to claim you as my own. You're my mate, Sky. Your sexy little body was made for me to pleasure and I'm going to show you exactly what that means."

My heart raced and I wanted to crawl up his big body and shake him. Or ride him. I couldn't decide which. It was awfully uncomfortable with the boys there.

I chose to keep my mouth shut. No sense trying to carry on a sane conversation with someone who was unbalanced. A dragon. Lord ha' mercy! God, why couldn't I just attract a normal man with a normal personality? A nice computer programmer or accountant, hell, even a pro-skateboarder or a dog walker would do, anyone who didn't claim he was a dragon.

"Just relax, little one. You'll understand it all eventually. We have all the time in the world."

It was laughable that he thought I might relax. The things he was saying, the way he spoke, the way he seemed to have no sense of propriety when it came to grabbing an unknown woman, calling her his and following her home... He was probably dangerous. He had to be dangerous. Yet, I found myself sinking into him again. Relaxing. *Letting* him hold me. And liking it.

"That's it. We'll be at your castle soon."

Oh, lord.

6

BEAST

My mate's castle was barely a shanty. It looked as though a heavy wind might crumble it to dust. That wouldn't do. There was no way she could remain there. If an enemy attempted to attack, they would need only to huff and puff to blow the structure down. I could not allow it. I could not allow her to remain somewhere unsafe, unguarded, somewhere she could be harmed.

When I told her that, she narrowed her eyes and glared at me with a nasty look, then stepped away from me like I was a smelly lump of dung stuck to her shoe. When her mouth half lifted in a snarl, it was clear that she didn't like my words, but I cared more about her protection than whether she was miffed by what I said. It was my duty to protect her. My castle was much safer.

When I told her that, too, she actually shoved me away before storming into the unlocked back door. *Unlocked!* I tried to follow her, but she turned on me and pointed up in my face. "Look. I've been nice so far, but this is ridiculous. You need to go on back home. You're pushy and rude and I don't care that you're hot. It doesn't make up for the fact that you're overbearing. And off your rocker." Her face became bright red and she slammed a flimsy door in my face. "Go. Away!"

I pushed the door and growled down at her shocked face after the flimsy thing fell off its hinges. "For some reason, your constant back-talk and sass turns me on."

"You're a psycho!" She watched me casually put her door down and then stomped her foot. "Go!"

The boys stood just inside in what I gathered was some sort of very small kitchen, staring out at us. The smaller one looked excited about his aunt being angry with me. When he caught me glaring at him, he snapped his gaze away and hurried out of the room. Nick stood trembling slightly, his back straight. He was trying to be brave and I felt myself admiring the young male. Frightened or not, he wasn't going to leave his aunt's side unless she forced him to.

"I am not leaving you here alone and unguarded. This house would not stand up to an attack. I broke your door down and I barely touched it."

"Well, you're a freak."

"A freak?"

She sighed and threw her hands up. "Whatever. If you want to sit out here and watch over the door that you just broke down, feel free. Could you try to keep the bugs out, too?"

"You would like me to stay?"

"I want you to go home, but you don't listen well." She went around and grabbed Nick's shoulder. "You and I are going to have a long talk tomorrow."

"Yes, ma'am."

They both disappeared and I stood wondering what the hell she expected me to do. Surely, she didn't really expect me to keep the bugs out all night. I was a dragon, not an exterminator. I put the door back, a little worse for the wear, and trailed along after her.

The hallway they'd gone down led to two rooms. Behind the door on the right, I could hear the boys arguing. Nick was angry at his little brother for getting him in trouble. Casey didn't seem to care. Behind the other door, I heard my mate settling into bed. Her intoxicating aroma beckoned me. I stepped into her room and pushed the door closed behind me.

"Oh, no you don't." Sky sat up in her bed. The blanket that fell to her waist revealed that she had removed her breast covering. Under her oversized shirt, her breasts hung free and swayed in a way that made my mouth water. "Get out of here!"

I shook my head and stepped closer. "I am getting tired of you telling me to leave. Why do you do it? I know you can feel that we are mates. I know that you feel attraction for me as I do for you. Why do you fight it?"

"First of all, I don't know what you're talking about with this *mate* business. What does that even mean to you? Second of all, you're a stranger who followed me home and is now standing in my bedroom uninvited, even though I'm telling you to get out. I should call the cops and have you arrested. I should." She pulled at her hair. "I don't even know why I'm not doing it. I should. I should just grab my phone and call 911. You're probably going to snap and murder us all in our sleep and it'll be all my fault because I didn't call for help. And all because I'm not thinking with the right part of my body."

I quickly stepped to her side and knelt. "I would never hurt you. I wouldn't hurt the young males, either, because you love them and that would hurt you. Even though the young male is rude to you."

"Nick isn't rude... He's just testing his boundaries."

"I didn't mean Nick." I shook my head. "Look at me. I'm on my knees. I would never hurt you. I would give you my sword and let you run it through my chest and pierce my heart before I hurt you."

"You have a sword? Why am I not surprised?"

"Every dragon has a sword."

"Why do you call yourself a dragon?"

"Because I am a dragon."

"You're not a dragon."

"I *am* a dragon."

"Prove it."

"You want me to show you *here*?"

She crossed her arms. "Yeah."

"Female, I am not some puny house dragon. I am a powerful, fierce fire-breathing, earth-shaking dragon. I would destroy your tiny shack if I shifted here. I would destroy your neighbor's shack, too."

Suddenly, she barked out a laugh. "Oh, I get it. This is about your penis size, isn't it? 'Big, earth-shaking dragon' is a metaphor. This whole thing is some weird penis joke? It's sooo big, you'd destroy me. Uh huh. Okay. That's great, *big* guy. I'm going to bed. Don't let the door hit ya' on the way out."

I sat back on my heels. "What? This is not about my penis."

"No, no, it's fine. I'm sure it's just massive. I'm just really tired and I have to be to work early."

"Little mate, you're irritating me."

She made a show of fluffing her pillows. "Well, we're even."

I stood up and glared down at her. "In my old world, I would not have even asked. You would have welcomed me. Begged me, perhaps."

"And in *my* old world, you'd have a really large penis *and* be sane. And you'd know how to use it. And you wouldn't be coming on so strong, but you wouldn't forget to call, either. And, you'd cook, clean, and know how to dance like the guys in Magic Mike."

I frowned. "What world are you from?"

"Shreveport."

"I don't understand anything you're saying, except that you wish me to have a big dick." I gestured to my pants. "I have a big dick. Can I get in bed with you now?"

She shook her head. "No! You're not getting in my bed."

I pressed my lips together and tried to think of a way to coax her to allow me to lie with her. I was tired but I wanted desperately to caress her soft, delicious little curvy body and hold it next to mine as we slept. She was being stubborn. "Come on, mate. I will hardly even touch you." I knew it would take only a couple well-placed strokes before I had her begging.

Even though she shook her head, she looked as though she wanted to smile. "Get out of here, Beast. Whoever named you that was wrong, by the way."

I scowled at her, suddenly ready to leave her room. "My mother named me that because she knew I'd be strong and rule over our kingdom. She was not wrong."

I left her in her bed, feeling like I'd just ended up punishing myself by walking away. Perhaps I should have tried harder. I did not know how to woo a human female. Had my mate been a dragon female, it would have been easy. I would not have had to do a thing. A dragon female would have begged, pleaded for me to claim her. I did not want a dragon female, though. I wanted my beautiful human mate.

Instead, I was lying on a tiny piece of furniture trying to figure out a way to position my large body on it in a more comfortable pose. It was old, saggy, and uncomfortable and things poked me from inside of it.

Then, I was awoken by some large mutant rodent purring at me from atop my chest. I pushed it off and shuddered. I had no cause to harm a small, non-threatening creature, but I wasn't fond of furry things that crept up while I slept. No sooner had the vile thing touched the ground, than it was back on my chest. It swatted at my face then settled in, getting comfortable while I stared at it.

It stared back with bright yellow eyes. The dark slits in the middle reminded me of a snake I'd known in the old world. That snake had had a nasty streak and I wondered if perhaps I should be more cautious. Perhaps I should destroy the tiny creature for the safety of my mate.

"Mate!" I bellowed out to her, hoping she could explain what the hell the thing on my chest was and whether it was of the harmful variety.

She came stumbling out of her room a few minutes later, her hair standing up and her eyes only half-opened. "What in the world are you shouting about?"

"What is this creature?"

She blinked a few times and then smiled. Her smile was so sweet and unguarded that I lost concern about the rodent on my chest and focused only on the blood rushing to my dick. "That's Bax. He normally stays outside at night. He must've got in through the door you busted down."

"What is a bax?"

She laughed. "He's a cat, silly."

I frowned. I'd heard of cats before. I'd even seen them. The thing on my chest was no cat. It was huge and it looked like something out of the horror movies Armand watched. "This is not a cat. This is some sort of deformed, mutant rodent."

She scooped the thing into her arms and held it against her chest. "That's not a very nice thing to say. He's just a little rough looking. He went up against a gator several years ago. He came out on top, but he has some battle scars."

Battle scars. I had those. That knowledge caused me to look at the little creature in a different light. "Okay. Put him back. He is a worthy companion, I guess."

She shook her head but put the creature back down on my chest. Her fingers grazed my bare chest as she did and I heard her suck in a breath. Instead of staying and exploring, though, she hurried away. Her door shut a second later and a lock clicked.

I chuckled. My female was cute. A lock, as though I couldn't easily level the entire house to get to her.

The little mutant settled back on my chest and purred when I touched its head the way Sky had. Maybe he wasn't so bad. Fierce little creature.

7
SKY

I woke up to the smell of...smoke! Something was burning! Thinking of the boys' safety, I shot out of bed and flew through the house. Instead of the boys, I found the unhinged stranger, Beast, standing in front of the stove staring at it like he wanted to smash it to pieces.

Eyeing him at the stove, every incredible hunky inch of him, brought back memories of the night before and I had to put my hand out to brace myself on the counter. He was still just as sexy. And still here. Yep, it wasn't a dream. I was still harboring a stark raving mad hottie.

"How do you work this contraption?" He glared at the stove, grabbed the cast iron skillet by the hot handle, and swore up a storm when it obviously burned his fingers. Tossing the skillet across the room, he slammed his fist down on the stove creating a severe crater down the middle of it.

Alarmed by his injury, I ignored my ruined stove and rushed over to grab his hand. His flesh was red and blistered, but as I watched, it faded back to normal skin like time-lapse videography.

I turned his massive hand over in mine, too focused to realize that touching him felt like sticking my tongue on a battery to test if it still had juice. His skin was rough and callused, rougher than I expected for a man who lived in a fancy house like his. What did he do for a living? I really hoped it wasn't illegal drug running or something.

His olive skin was dusted with dark hair that matched the dark waves on his head. He had beautiful hands. Masculine, strong. Strong enough to crush my stove. Strong enough to lift me as if I'd weighed nothing.

"The burn..." I looked up at him. "Where'd it go?"

Standing that close to him was a mistake. He was devastating that close. I could see the colors of his eyes, black with glittery flecks of gold that seemed to burn and glow, the stubble covering his jaw and chin, the softness of his mouth. A scar ran through one of his eyebrows and stood out, paler against the darker tone of his skin, another on that soft upper lip.

"I told you. I am a dragon. We heal. Fast." He caught my fingers in his and pulled me into his hard chest. "Good morning, sweet little mate. I tried to make you breakfast."

My insides swooned. It was stupid and weak, getting all jelly-legged because a man tried, unsuccessfully, to cook me breakfast—then broke my stove. The bar was low, apparently, and swoon I did. *Internally*. Externally, I tried my best to hide what the feel of his chest pressed against mine did to me. Judging by the growl emanating from Beast's throat and the giant rod poking me in the stomach, I didn't think he was oblivious to my swooning. Or maybe he was doing swooning of his own.

"I think I shall have *you* for breakfast, instead." His deep voice was intense, full of promises. His hands took my sides, the soft parts of my body that I'd rather no one touched, and squeezed as he pulled me even harder into his chest.

My mouth opened, whether to tell him to stop or to moan, I wasn't sure. I was instantly acutely aware of that strange buzzing. Energy, intense, right before the point of stinging, sizzled between us.

"What's he still doing here?" Nick's angry voice cut through my lust-fog and sent me tumbling away from Beast.

I almost toppled straight to the ground, but Beast caught me and righted me. I smoothed down my night shirt and moved back towards my bedroom. "Be nice, Nick. You're the one who went trampling through his property uninvited. And illegally, I might add."

"He's..." Nick shook his head. "I think he's dangerous, Aunt Sky."

Beast shrugged and puffed out his chest. "I *am* dangerous."

I cut my eyes to him. "Not helping."

"I mean... He's not like us. He's a..." Nick stopped himself and looked around. "God, this is so crazy."

Casey strolled into the room and looked around. "It's not crazy. He's a dragon."

I groaned and ran my hands through my hair. "Okay. I'm going to go get dressed and then I'll take you guys to school."

"No way. We can take ourselves." Casey's eyebrows furrowed. "What happened to the stove?"

"Nothing." I kept my eyes away from Beast, afraid of the look I'd see on his face. How had he convinced the boys that he was a dragon? "How do I know that you won't leave school? Or just not show up at all?"

"Maybe you should just trust us?"

"Trust you? After the stunt you pulled last night?"

"Jeez, Sky, don't have a freak out."

Beast growled, loudly, and, for the briefest of seconds, I wondered about the whole dragon thing. "I may not have the pleasure of eating you for an afternoon snack, but I will still make you suffer if you talk to my mate like that."

"Can you *not* threaten my nephews, please?"

"The small male started it. He is disrespectful to you. He deserves to be upended and spanked like the baby he is."

"I'm not a fucking baby!" Casey's outburst shocked the room. His hands were balled into fists at his sides and there was a dark scowl on his face.

I couldn't believe what I was seeing. Casey, in that moment, didn't look anything like the little boy I'd brought into my house six years prior. He looked like his father—angry and raging, ready to tear apart the world for whatever injustices, real or perceived, he felt had been thrust upon him. "*Stop it, Casey.*"

"*You* stop it!" He shook, his small body vibrating with rage and whatever other extreme emotions were surging through him.

"Casey…" Nick stepped forward, but Casey shoved him away.

"I'm sick of both of you! I hate you. I hate everything here!" He tried to run past me but I stepped in front of him and wrapped my arms around him. "Get off of me! Get off! I hate you!"

I held him tighter, even as his fists landed a rain of punches on my stomach and sides. "Stop it, Casey. This isn't you. We can't behave this way. We have to talk and work things out. We're a family."

Casey was suddenly yanked away from me and suspended in the air. Beast glared at him and shook him when Casey tried to strike him, too. "Why do you treat the female caring for you that way? Does she not feed you? Does she not give you a room and a home with your brother? What would make you think that it is a wise choice to talk to her like that? What would make you think that it is a wise choice to strike her?"

I put a hand on Beast's arm and fought back tears. I didn't know why things were falling apart all of a sudden. I supposed they had always been skating the edge of collapse, or at least explosion—but this? Casey's behavior was shocking. I still didn't want Beast to actually shake him senseless, though.

"No, you will not defend him right now. Not after he just laid his hands on you. I will fight my every instinct to bite his little head off, but you must stand back and let the young male answer."

I stepped back, unsure of my place in my own house. As much as Beast talked about hurting Casey, somehow I knew instinctually that he wouldn't actually do it. Which was stupid. How could I possibly know what an unbalanced stranger who followed me home and wouldn't leave would do—in any situation? Maybe *I* was behaving unbalanced. I didn't know Beast. He'd just let himself into my house and there I was, suddenly co-parenting with him.

"I want to go home!" Casey screamed it at the top of his lungs, tears filling his eyes. "If dragons can exist, then I should be able to get my dad back. And my mom. I want them back. I don't want to live here!"

My heart broke into a million pieces for the little boy in front of me. He acted so tough most of the time, so beyond his years, that I'd forgotten that he was just a kid. He still had baby fat on his cheeks that made them preciously round. He believed in dragons, for Christ's sake. He was wandering, lost. We were all wandering lost.

8
SKY

Beast lowered Casey to the floor and rested his hands on his shoulders. "Where are your parents?"

Casey said nothing. It was Nick who spoke. "Gone. Our mom left when we were little and Dad's in prison." Nick stepped forward and shoved Casey. "And he's not getting out. Mom's not coming back, either. Get it through your head. You want to go back to foster care? Don't mess up what we have here because you think you can wish them back."

Casey covered his face with his hands and sobbed, his whole body shaking with the effort.

I snapped into action, realizing I'd gone comatose for too long. I grabbed him and pulled him into my chest again. When Nick sighed from behind him, I grabbed him, too. I held them both to me and tried my best to keep myself together. I did suck at this.

How did single moms do it? I felt as though I was treading water and the undertow kept tugging, threatening to drag me below the surface. And it was only getting worse. Now that the boys were in their teens, becoming young men, I was responsible for not only playing the role of mom, for which I was ill equipped, but also trying to ease their transition into manhood by being a substitute for the dad that was no longer around.

At twenty-nine, trying to raise two teenagers felt an awful lot like an insurmountable task on the good days. Today was not one of the good days. I didn't have a choice, though. They needed me and I loved them. I would never abandon them. So, I held them tighter and took deep breaths to calm myself.

Finally, Nick pulled back. "We have to get to school."

Casey wiped his eyes and pulled away, too. He didn't say anything to me, just grabbed his backpack and walked out the door. Nick squeezed my arm as he hurried past me to follow his brother.

"I love you guys." As usual, I received no response. I slumped against the counter and blew out a ragged breath. I was at a loss when it came to them. I wanted desperately to make their lives better, but I was afraid I was just messing things up for them up even more.

"You are sad." Beast heaved a big sigh and moved towards me. "I'll fix it."

I looked over at him and forced a smile. "If you suggest killing them or eating them one more time, I'm going to scream."

He cupped my face in his hands and stared down at me with a sincerity that took my breath away. "No. No killing. The young males are okay. I don't like when they aren't kind to you, but that will change. I will make sure."

"Why are you here?"

"I told you. You are mine. Do you think I would find you simply to let you go? Is that how do humans do it?"

When he asked about humans *doing it*, my face burned. Lord ha' mercy, I was acting like some hormone-ravaged teenager. The fact was, I couldn't tell him how humans did it. I didn't really know. I'd never *done it*. I was, embarrassingly, a twenty-nine year old virgin. Not exactly by choice. It had just happened.

It had been years since I'd dated. I hadn't had time since the boys arrived. And, for several years before that, I'd been so completely immersed in tracking them down, both living with different foster care families. Then, once I found them, there was the struggle of trying to gain custody of both of them. Dealing with lawyers, the courts, not to mention working extra shifts to pay for it all, ate up all my time and energy. There was never time for romantic relationships. I was lucky if I had time for a full night's sleep.

He lowered his mouth and pressed his lips against my cheek. "You are warm. Are you okay? Why is your face heating like this?"

If there was ever a time for a hole to open up in the floor, it was then. "I'm fine." Who was this sex-starved hussy taking over my body every time Beast was near?

He easily lifted me and put me down on the counter, stepping between my thighs and wrapping his arms around my waist. "I don't like you being sad. I want to make it change. Tell me how."

I put my hands against his chest, intending to push him away, but nothing happened. My wrists refused to put any power into the movement and I ended up just caressing him. "Sometimes, people are just sad. Overwhelmed is a better word, I guess."

"I will fix it."

"You keep saying that."

He nodded, his unusual eyes intent on mine. "I am a strong warrior. If I can't defeat your sadness, then I don't deserve you as my mate."

I let my head fall back to rest against the cabinet. "This is too much."

"What do you mean?"

"You. You thinking you're some kind of warrior dragon. The boys. I'm too young to parent them and too old to believe you." I finally managed to push him away and hopped off the counter scurrying out of the kitchen, heading to my bedroom. "You have to go. As interesting as this, uh, *visit*, has been, I have the real world to get back to. I have a job. I have bills. Real life isn't a fairytale with castles and imaginary dragons."

"You're starting to frustrate me again."

I spun on him and threw my hands up. "Are you serious? *I'm* frustrating *you*?"

"Yes!" He grabbed my arms and yanked me against him. "You're acting like you don't know that we are meant for one another, as though you don't feel it throughout every morsel of your being. Every time I look at you, my cock hardens, my heart races and my mouth waters. You know why I react that way, little one? Because you are *mine*. I am *yours*. You know this. I can scent you. You are wet for me. Even now, you are aroused—for me."

Equally horrified and turned on, I yanked away from him and stalked into my bedroom. "You are completely bonkers!"

He was there, grabbing me again, only this time it was his front to my back. "Why are you fighting this?"

Breathing heavily, I felt my whole world caving in to just that moment. It didn't make any sense, but his hands on me, him touching me, it made everything stop. All the questions and concerns I had about some psychotic stranger just inserting himself into my life and grabbing me like I belonged to him, all of the worries I had, all the responsibilities, they all just faded. Everything melted until all that remained was his touch, just Beast, just him.

"You're mine, little one." His words were barely more than a growl in my ear before he spun me around and his mouth descended on mine, his tongue parting my lips.

It wasn't my first kiss, but it was the first time I'd *really* been kissed, a kiss with truth and passion behind it. He held my head with one hand and my hips with the other, keeping me where he wanted me as he tasted and explored with his tongue. Slow and intense, it was a kiss meant to make me forget everything, including my own name. I knew that I was being seduced with a kiss, and I was all in.

I gripped his shirt at his waist, trying to ground myself otherwise I was going to float right away. His hard body under the shirt was just more temptation, though. His tongue tangling with mine had my feet leaving the ground.

I pulled back with a start as I realized my feet actually were leaving the ground. Beast held my ass cheeks in his hands and stared at me through heavy-lidded eyes. A hungry look, as though he wanted nothing more than to devour me whole. My legs were wrapped around his waist, my ankles locked tightly behind his back. I didn't even know how that happened. What was I doing...

"Come back, mate. Don't allow your mind to leave us." He moved back and sat on the edge of my bed. Then his mouth was on my neck and he was stretching out my shirt to kiss down my collar bone. "You taste even better than I imagined."

I tipped my head back, white-hot desire shooting through me and I was eager to feel more of what he was doing. That had never happened before. I'd read about sizzling passion in romance books, seen a few soft-porn movies that tried hard to depict it, but I'd never felt it. It was fucking amazing. His lips were soft and hot and demanding, his beard stubble, rough. The mix of it had me wiggling on his lap. Suddenly a thought popped into my head and I laughed. "You thinking about me, too, huh?"

A deep rumbling laugh from him had me blushing as I realized what I'd boldly asked. He tilted his head back and grinned. The sight was breath-taking. His straight teeth parted as his tongue brushed over his lips. "Nonstop."

I didn't want to open my mouth and say anything, but I had to before things got too far, and I had a feeling this might just go too far. "I've never... I've never *done it* before." I shuddered. "I've never done anything before..."

"Good. You were not made for other males. You are for me. For the one who will protect you, cherish you, and adore you. For the male who treasures you."

9

BEAST

I knew she was a virgin. A dragon's mate always is. Still, hearing her say the words ignited an even hotter flame in me. I was going to be hers and make her mine. She'd wear my mark and carry my scent, identifiable to anyone else who ever drew near her. No other male would ever dare lay a finger on her lest they lose their arm. I would fight to the death to defend her, and it would not be *my* death.

"I shall pleasure you, little one, and I will savor every moment." I bit down harder on her shoulder, leaving a temporary mark. She responded like magic.

When I dragged her hips harder into mine and my cock pressed against her, she dug her nails into my shoulders and threw her head back. "Beast..."

I growled and ripped the shirt off her. "Say it again."

She gasped as the shredded fabric fell to the floor in pieces and she was revealed to me in just a simple beige breast covering. It was slightly darker than her skin and held her heavy breasts in a way that I envied. I wanted to cup them like that. With one slip of a claw, I removed the contraption and it sprung open.

"Beast!" That time my name sounded more accusatory than I

liked. Sky wrapped her arm over her breasts and checked out her breast covering with the other hand. "Bras aren't cheap, you know? This was my last good bra. What were you thinking?"

"Remain calm. I have all the money we could ever need. I shall buy another. I shall buy you whatever you wish."

I knew it was the wrong thing to say when she shoved my shoulder and climbed off my lap. I sat pouting, wondering what I had done.

She kept her breasts covered as she stalked to the other side of the bedroom, still gripping the torn covering. Her bare back was smooth and lovely. The curve of it was more than enough to keep my eyes riveted and my cock painfully hard. I wanted to run my tongue down the ridges of her spine and dip lower to taste every part of her.

"Stop looking at me like that. You can't just ruin my undergarments and think that it's okay."

"I'll buy you new ones. I'll buy you all the breast coverings in this world, if you'll just come back here."

"This is crazy. I'm crazy for letting myself getting carried away with you."

I wasn't having that kind of talk. I got up and stalked over to her, lifting her into my arms and bit my lip as she exposed her beautiful breasts to me. She responded by catching me around the neck. Her legs came up around my thighs, trapping me against her.

"There is nothing crazy about wanting to give yourself to me. There is nothing crazy about *us*." I pressed my lips to hers and felt the tension leave my chest as she didn't resist. I'd never been a fan of kissing before. It didn't seem to make much sense. Why press mouths together as though pretending to be some species of strange, sucking fish? With Sky, I couldn't get enough. The feel of her silky smooth lips, velvety tongue, the very taste of her, sent passion soaring to a whole new level.

Her arms clung tightly to me; her chest pressed into mine. Her hands gripped at my hair and tugged. "Beast. What is this?"

I kissed down her throat, tasting her sweet, soft skin and lifted her higher as I trailed my mouth down her chest. Capturing one of her small pink nipples in my mouth, I stroked it with my tongue before biting gently and sucking.

Sky arched in my arms, thrusting her chest into my face. She cried out and tugged harder at my hair. "Beast!"

I moved to her other nipple and worked back and forth, making her squirm with pleasure until I couldn't take anymore. The smell of her arousal surrounded me, intoxicating me. I felt drunk yet needed more. I dropped to my knees and shredded her pants and underwear. This time, she said nothing about it. Lifting her thighs onto my shoulder, I was helpless to stop, unable to give her time to adjust to what was happening before I buried my face into her core.

She tasted so indescribably delicious that I licked her over and over savoring her sweetness, then buried my tongue inside her. More of her juices flowed and I lapped it up. It was my duty, my honor, to pleasure my mate. I sucked her little bud into my mouth and gently stroked it while slowly circling her entrance with my finger.

Mere seconds passed before she tightened and cried out. Her essence leaked onto my finger and I growled with the urge to stand up and thrust my cock into her. I buried my face into the crook of her thigh and then sank my teeth into her soft flesh, leaving another mark.

"Beast...shit!"

She wasn't ready for me to enter her, yet. She was small and tight and I was very large. It was my privilege to have such a fine and beautiful mate, and it was not only my obligation, but my sheer delight to prepare her in every way.

I looked up at her and licked my lips. "You taste fucking divine. I could feast on you all day long, little mate."

She gave an uncomfortable laugh and attempted to slip her hand over herself to hide from my view. "Put me down, please."

I nipped her fingers and grinned up at her. "I am not done with you yet."

"I already came. That's enough, Beast. You don't have—" Her voice cut off when I lowered my mouth to her bud again. Then, it rang higher when I pushed my finger into her, stroking the hot, velvet walls of her core as I did. "Beast!"

I sucked harder and pushed in another finger, stretching her. I sensed her already close to coming apart on my tongue and fingers again. It filled my chest with joy. My mate was responsive and opening herself to me, allowing me to pleasure her and the pride I felt was like nothing I'd ever experienced.

When she climaxed that time, on my fingers, her body tensed and shuddered, squeezing me. Her muscles milked my fingers in a pulsing rhythm that made my mouth water.

I gave her another break, leaving my fingers inside her, lightly stroking my tongue over her bud every little bit, just keeping her on the edge for as long as possible. When she regained enough of her senses to speak, I started all over again. Another finger, a different pattern with my tongue. Curling my fingers, sucking on the sensitive little bud. Thrusting slow and gentle, lightly scraping her with my teeth. Thrusting hard and fast, sucking harder. Another finger, stretching her until her nails scratched my skin, drawing blood to the surface. Pumping in and out through her orgasms. Stroking the little rose at the back of her slit, drinking her come as she fell apart again and again.

I didn't know how long I'd been tasting and pleasuring my female. Time was of no consequence to me. Sky was the most amazing female I had ever seen, and I could not get enough of her incredible flavor. But, when she finally went limp, I knew that she'd had enough for the time being. I tenderly licked her clean while her body shuddered against me, and then lifted her into my arms and held her close while I carried her into her bathroom.

Her tub was small, but after filling it with hot water, I squeezed us both into it. I held her and stroked her body, just enjoying the extraordinary mate this world had granted me with.

My cock ached and I wanted very badly to bury myself in her, but she was delicate and it was up to me to care for her needs before my own. I would not rush her. I had forever with her. As much as it hurt to ignore my throbbing dick, I desired her pleasure more than my own.

Unable to contain myself, I reached my arm around and stroked her to another orgasm in the bath. She was too alluring. She awakened every instinct in me and drove me fucking crazy. After I'd had a taste, I knew that I'd never get enough of her.

10

SKY

Amie's eyebrows raised questioningly when I walked in three hours late with Beast trailing behind me. Her look wasn't so much a question as it was an astonished expression of pure amazement. I wasn't sure if it was because of me, or because of Beast.

He'd insisted on coming to work with me. After countless orgasms, washing me in the bath, and watching me as I got dressed, staring at me with so much heat and intensity in his gaze that I almost melted, I couldn't argue with him too much. I'd lost my ability to speak. I'd almost lost my ability to walk.

I could still feel his mouth on me, his fingers in me. Orgasms with my vibrator had never been so amazing. If I'd only know what I'd been missing. Although, something told me that Beast was different from other men. In so many ways.

Beast caught my arm and tugged me back against his chest. Looking down at me, he trailed his eyes down to my chest and gave a little growl. "Your heart is racing the same way it does when I touch you. Are you sure you don't wish to go back home and finish what we started?"

I felt my face go fifty shades of red and put my hand on his chest.

Under that shirt, he'd had deep scratches. Scratches that had healed by the time he put the shirt back on. I still didn't know what was up with that. "I have to work."

He bent down and kissed me. "Too bad."

I stumbled back a step as he let me go and watched him walk over to an empty booth. Settling into it, he picked up the menu and looked it over.

I turned to Amie who was staring with wide eyes. Seeing her really cemented the fact that since the last time I'd been here, not even twenty-four hours prior, my love life, or lack of it, had done a complete one-eighty. I was on someone else's rollercoaster ride.

She grabbed my arm and pulled me towards the back. "What the fuck is going on?"

I opened my mouth and found that I didn't know what to say. I closed it and then opened it again. "Um..."

She gestured towards the front of the café. "Who the hell is that gorgeous morsel of stud muffin and what are you doing with him? Last I checked, you were single."

I shrugged. "I don't know."

"What do you mean you don't know? He just kissed the shit out of you and the look he gave you melted *my* panties."

I dizzied a little and leaned against the counter behind me. "Yeah... He does that."

"You look like you've just been fucked good and well for hours. I need to know everything. Details, chère."

Marcus stepped out of his office and glared at me. "You're late."

"I know. I'm sorry. I was..." I couldn't think of anything to say other than I was having multiple orgasms at Beast's hands and mouth.

"Getting fucked." Amie whispered behind a cough.

"I don't want to know. Don't let it happen again." He scowled and shook his head. "Now, get to work. And stop smiling so damn much."

I hadn't even realized I was grinning. I straightened my face and nodded. "Sure thing."

Amie followed me into the main room and hissed behind me.

"You're not getting away without giving me details. Now, get busy. I've been covering you, but I'll gladly give you the tips if you take over for tables five and six."

I looked over at the table of perfectly coiffed women holding clipboards and talking animatedly. "Oh, no."

Amie laughed. "Oh, yes. Something I'm sure you've been shouting a lot this morning."

I swatted at her, but she moved out of range and skirted off to other tables leaving me with the PTA moms. I would've recognized them anywhere. They were all put together with their perfect highlighted hair and their perfect manicures and their perfect designer clothes and their perfectly judgmental sneers. Even in a small school district like the one we were in, the PTA was like a mini mafia. Possibly even darker than the real mafia.

I stopped at their table and noticed they still had menus in front of them. "Are you gals ready to order or do you need a little longer?"

The one in charge, clearly an obvious choice due to her having the biggest hair and thickest false eyelashes, glanced at me disdainfully and raised her eyebrows. "We've *been* ready."

I kept my smile in place. "Wonderful. I'll go ahead and take those orders now so we can get your food out to you as soon as possible."

She sighed heavily and rolled her eyes. "Fine. I'll have an egg white and spinach omelet, fresh spring water and half of an avocado."

I took the rest of the table's tasteless orders before smiling at them and starting to walk away. The clearing of a throat stopped me. I looked back and saw the head 'bitch in charge' scowling at me.

"Are you going to take these menus, or what?"

I heard the low growl from Beast's direction and winced. "Of course. So sorry. I'll get those out of your way."

"Did that man just growl?" She nodded at Beast and I witnessed the instant she *really* saw him. She sat up straighter, pushed her breasts forward and released a breathy whisper. "Oh, wow."

I felt a pang of jealously and had to fight to keep it under wraps. Moving away from their table, I dropped their order ticket off to the kitchen and paused to take a deep, calming breath. I barely had a second to calm myself before I had to hurry back out and take a few more orders

When I was finally able to check on Beast, I felt the same fluttering in my stomach that he always gave me. I rested my order pad on my hip and nodded to his menu. "Anything acceptable for a beast to eat?"

His eyes trailed slowly down my body. "Oh, yes."

I fought a blush and shook my head. "What do you want to eat?"

"Same answer."

"Beast." I crossed my arms over my chest and bit my lip. It was hard to focus with him around. I hadn't even started to tackle the question of *why* he was around.

"*Sky*."

An unexpected zing of lust rippled through me and I had to grab the edge of his table to steady myself. "Don't do that."

"Don't say your name?" He tapped his fingers on the table and licked his lips. "Or don't say your name like I'm imaging what your little body is going to feel like wrapped around my cock?"

I snatched his menu away from him and smacked him with it before I even thought twice about it. The heated look he gave me was dangerous.

"You want me to bend you over and redden your sweet ass, don't you?"

Someone at the table behind him coughed and I hit him with the menu on the arm again. "Stop it! I work here, Beast. I have to come back here tomorrow and the next day and the next."

"No, you don't." He shrugged. "What time do the young males get home?"

My stomach fluttered. "They come here after school and then we go home together. Unless they sneak off in the search of a swamp monster slash dragon."

"So, we have to wait until tonight. That will not be easy."

I just walked away. I didn't know what to do with him. I didn't even understand why he was still following me around. It didn't make any sense. Yet, at some level, it also felt natural and easy to let him touch me and demand things from my body. *Just which one of us was the crazy one?*

I put in an order for Beast and then made myself busy serving meals and cleaning tables. When I took the food to the PTA ladies, they were just as rude as ever, each of them finding something about the food to complain about after their queen bitch did.

The orange juice was too pulpy, the avocados didn't taste like they'd been picked up at the market that morning, the egg whites were tasteless. Egg whites tasteless, imagine that! It was infuriating, but I dealt with their type daily.

My overbearing 'wannabe dragon' didn't, though. His low growl had turned into something a little louder, a little fiercer. When he started to get out of his seat, I held up my hands to ward him off and shot him a sharp glare. Amazingly, he remained seated.

After nodding my head and pretending to take notes from the PTA witches on how their orders should have properly been prepared, I hurried to the kitchen, dropped off a couple more order tickets to the cook and picked up Beast's food. When I placed it in front of him, I smiled sweetly.

"Can you be a good dragon and sit here nicely without growling at the other diners?"

He growled at me and snapped his arm out to grab me and pull me into his booth. He brushed his lips over the shell of my ear and nipped it. "I'm ready to go home."

I shivered with pleasure, but still pulled myself away. "Finally. Go home, then. I'm busy."

"I will not leave without you. Especially not with those women treating you like that. If they only knew. You are the mate of a warrior dragon. You are deserving of respect. They should be falling at your feet. You should not be serving them like some house maid."

Embarrassed and angry, I put my hands on my hips and backed away. "You're an asshole, you know that."

Almost comically, he threw his hands up and groaned. "You are confusing. What did I say now?"

"I'm not a house maid. I'm a *waitress*. This is my job. It might be beneath you, Mr. High-and-mighty, but it's how I support my family."

"*I'm* your family."

I gave a growl of my own. "This is too much. *You're* too much. You're completely bananas. Finish your food; it's on me. Then, go home. Without me."

11

BEAST

I wasn't going anywhere without her. She was stuck with me, no matter what. I glared at the women who were being rude to Sky. My mate was too nice. With the food in front of me, I picked up a piece of fried fish and examined it. Dragon females of the old world wouldn't have stood for that type of treatment. They fought for and demanded the respect they deserved.

Sky was soft. I took a bite of the fish and watched as she crossed the room with an armload of plates. Soft, but strong. I couldn't deny that her softness did things to me, too. Seeing the way she cared for the young males, even when they behaved as selfish younglings, made me think of the way she'd be with our younglings. She would love them, probably too much. They'd probably end up soft but strong like her. For some reason, that made me smile.

I huffed and shoved the rest of the fish into my mouth. It seemed like I was the only person she wanted to be direct with. In my opinion, she should've kicked the nasty women out long before me.

After my food was gone, I stayed and waited for her to come back around to me. It appeared as though she was intent on ignoring me, though. I wasn't used to the feeling, and I found myself wanting to stand up and demand her attention. I was her mate. Who could be more interesting than one's mate? Human women didn't make much sense to me. I had a lot to learn.

Time crawled and I was too old to start letting time get to me, so I stood up and approached Sky. She barely looked at me and it drove me crazy. "Female, what is wrong with you?"

She walked away and dropped a drink off before coming back to where I stood. "Don't call me female."

"You should be nicer to your mate." I crossed my arms over my chest, thinking that she'd realize that I was right.

Instead, she raised her eyebrows at me in that infuriating way that told me I was about to see just how much attitude she could dish out. "I thought I asked you to leave."

I frowned. "I am not leaving. Not without you."

"What are you just gonna sit there and watch me work all day?" She tried to walk away, but I caught her arm.

"Little one, stop. We can go home and get back to the good stuff. It was much more fun than anger."

She bared her teeth at me, letting me see that she possessed all of the strength that I could ever want in a mate. I didn't doubt that she'd try to bite me any moment. "You're stressing me out. I can't focus with you here. And I've had enough of your judgmental attitude. About my kids, my house, my job. This is my life. *You* walked into *it*. If you don't like it, there's the door. Please use it."

"Your kids are troubled. Your house is falling down. And you don't have to work anymore. You have a mate who is a very wealthy dragon." I was getting tired of fighting with her. I just wanted sex and some cuddling with her. I'd never tried cuddling before but it seemed like something I would like—as long as it was with her.

"You are not a fucking dragon!" Her raised voice drew the stares of the people around us and a man came out of the back to scowl at us.

Fed up, I caught her arm and pulled her to me. "We will go to my castle and solve this right now. We will not have disagreements and resentments between us"

Her friend came over and gave Sky a look. "Marcus is getting pissed. Go take care of whatever you need to and I'll cover for you today."

Sky pushed me away and took the woman's hand. "Are you sure? I just need to…"

"Yes. Go. You can cover for me tomorrow. I'm going to a specialist about the thing."

"Shit. Okay, of course." Sky hugged her friend and then glared back at me. "Okay, let's go, *dragon*."

I took her hand and pulled her out of the café. She was still trying to get her apron off, but I was in a hurry to get this resolved and out of the way. I was tired of her doubting me.

"Wait, Beast! How are we getting there?"

I gave her a wicked grin. "Flying."

She stopped walking and scowled at me. "I'm over this."

I easily scooped her up and tossed her over my shoulder before speeding out of there. I hurried back to her house with her bouncing all the way, then slipped into the water behind it.

"What are you doing?! No! Don't go into the water; are you crazy? What am I saying, of course you're crazy!"

Her heart pounded a thunderous beat against my back as I went deeper still. "We won't be in it for long. I just need to get to the other side. We need more privacy."

She fought me, but I just moved faster, at one point, swimming and dragging her with me. When I got to the other side of the water, I carried her through the tall brush and stopped only when we reached a clearing.

She was livid when I put her down. "What is wrong with you?! The water is dangerous!"

"*I'm* dangerous."

"I'm starting to agree with you." She turned away and ran her fingers over her wet hair. "Look, Beast, this has to stop. I have enough problems with my life as it is. I can't….I mean, you're hot as Hades and for some damned reason, I get so turned on around you I can barely think straight, but you obviously come with a whole shit ton of issues. This—whatever it is—between you and me, is the last thing I need. It's the last thing the boys need. I'm going to go home, Beast. I'm done."

I left her standing there with her arms folded over her chest and backed away far enough to not crush her when I shifted. Then, I stripped my clothes off and winked at her before allowing my dragon form to emerge.

The feeling was always refreshing. Slipping into my dragon form was pure power and strength. Black scales covered my oversized body, hard as diamonds, matte and edged in gold. They created quite the magnificent sight, if I did say so myself. I stretched my long, leathery wings out and whipped my tail. Lifting my head, I released a puff of fire just for show and, of course, to impress my female, and then looked down for her reaction.

She stood far below me, her mouth hanging open, her eyes wide. Ha! She was impressed. I knew it. She appeared amazed by what she was seeing. If I expected her to scream, I'd have been wrong, though. She moved closer.

Pride reared in me. People didn't usually move towards me. I was terrifyingly large and I radiated power that intimidated most. My soft, strong mate, though, she moved in closer. Her hand stretched out and she stroked the scales on my foot.

"Holy shit."

I chuffed, wishing for the first time that I could laugh in dragon form. I wanted to talk to her. Eventually, when we'd fully mated and been together for a bit longer, we'd be able to communicate through our telepathy as dragons could with one another. Until then, I'd have to get creative to communicate with her.

I knelt in front of her, resting my head on the ground and looked back at my neck trying to coax her to crawl on. I'd never had someone ride me before, but it was a first I was looking forward to. I belonged to her as much as she belonged to me and I wanted her to experience my world, a little taste of it, anyway.

She gave me a wide eyed look. "You want me to crawl onto you?"

I chuffed again and nodded my head.

"Holy shit. This is insane." She did as I wanted, though. She crawled onto my body and her legs straddled my neck. Her arms wrapped around as far as they would go and her face pressed against the back of my head.

I had the inane thought that I may have to get her some sort of saddle to keep her safe if it was something we wanted to do very often. I didn't want to chance her getting hurt if she slipped, and the way she felt astride me, I knew I would want to do it often.

With that thought in mind, I lifted into the air slower than normal so as not to startle her. I went higher and higher, until I'd appear just a large bird from the ground. Sky's heart pounded against my neck. She smelled of fear, but under that fear, I was shocked to find that she scented of arousal. I had to smile. That was my female.

12

SKY

The truth that Beast wasn't actually some hot but pathetic crazy man like I'd thought sunk in more and more as we soared through the sky. The moment we landed in the open swamp by his house, I knew what I wanted. I'd known it in the air, too. Flying so high above everything, looking down at the world like it was this tiny thing, it had terrified me, but also left me invigorated. I wanted to touch the man again. The dragon was hypnotic and astonishing, but I wanted the man back under my fingers so I could give in to what my body demanded.

I slid off Beast's back and splashed into the water forgetting all about snapping alligators and poisonous snakes. I had a dragon beside me. Surely, he'd scare away any piddly little gator or copperhead. The dock was just a few feet away, and I didn't waste any time getting to it. I started to hoist myself up and felt hands wrap around my waist lifting me out of the water.

I spun around and came face to face with Beast, now a very large, very sexy, very naked man. His handsome face was wet and wild-eyed. His dark hair flopped over his forehead. We stared at each other for a few seconds. I suddenly saw him in a whole new light now that I knew he wasn't crazy. Maybe the world was crazy, I mean—dragons!

But he really was who and what he claimed. And, I wanted him like I'd never wanted anyone or anything before. I wasn't exactly sure how to go about it. Things like passion and seduction were all new to me. It suddenly seemed as though the entire world was new to me.

He looked at me with a concerned expression. "Are you—"

I decided that, like him, I would just take what I wanted. Before he could finish his sentence, I grabbed his face, stood on my tip toes and kissed him hard. Not enough. I jumped up and hooked my legs around his waist. He caught my ass in his hands and squeezed as I kissed him harder, slipping my tongue into his mouth. I wanted to make him feel the way I'd felt when he kissed me. Nipping and sucking his lips, I let myself go.

He was naked and as I moaned into his mouth, I stroked my hands over his shoulders and back. I dug my fingers in trying to pull him even closer to me.

The big man who harbored a big dragon that flew through the sky and who bragged about how powerful he was, stumbled because of me. We went down in a heap, Beast catching me so I hit the wooden dock with barely more than a slight bump. He stared down at me with those gold flecks in his eyes glowing brighter.

I thought about how they matched the gold on his big dragon body. He was stunning. In each of his forms I was intoxicated by him.

"I want to consummate our mating, little one." His voice was gruffer, just above a growl and it sent shivers all over my wet body.

I locked my fingers in his hair and dragged his mouth down to mine sucking his bottom lip gently. Then, I moved to his ear, nibbling on the lobe. "What are you waiting for?"

I wasn't even sure how it happened, but I was suddenly naked and my work clothes were floating away in the bayou, but I didn't care. I was so focused on the feeling of Beast resting his naked body against mine. I felt the heaviness of his cock pressing against my thigh and moaned. I should have been frightened. Or, maybe embarrassed to have never had sex before. It was time. I was going to lose my virginity to a dragon on a boat dock. If that didn't beat all! And, it felt right, so I didn't even stop to second guess it.

Beast must've read my mind, though. He stood up and held me in his arms, tightly against his chest, while heading towards his house. "Bed. I will take you to my bed."

I kissed his neck and whispered in his ear how much I wanted him while he walked. Pulling at his hair and doing my best to rub my chest against his, I felt like a fire had been lit in me. I knew how good he could make me feel and I wanted more. I wanted to make him feel that good, too.

"Fuck. I can't wait, Sky." He settled into a big chair on his patio and positioned me on top of him. "I need to be one with you."

Sitting on his lap, my thighs spread wide open, I was completely on display. His eyes raked over my chest and then my pussy, drinking me in. The way he looked at me, I'd never felt more beautiful. I wanted him to look. I felt like I'd gone wild. I stretched my arms above my head and bit my lip as he growled.

His big hands captured my breasts and tweaked my nipples before one of his hands trailed down my stomach and cupped my core. His palm pressed against my clit and his fingers played against my folds. "Are you sure you're ready?"

I nodded. "Yes. Do it. Please"

His fingers dipped lower and spread my folds. The tip of him pressed against me and I held my breath. As his head pushed into me, I gasped at how amazing it felt. The pressure of it was intense as more of him slowly eased into me. My body stretched and pulsed around him. Holy crap. He felt incredible.

"Okay?"

I nodded and then cried out as I was filled even more. I gripped his shoulders and blew out a rough breath before forcing myself down on him. Sinking until my thighs rested against his, I could feel him in what seemed like every single nerve ending of my body. He was fully inside me and I wasn't sure whether I wanted to beg him to be still or beg him to start moving.

My heart pounded and when I met Beast's eyes, my world altered. For a moment, I felt every crazy thing he'd been telling me down to my very soul. Mate. Dragon. I was meant for him. We were made for each other.

His eyes glowed, the gold flecks shimmering. His hands gripped my ass and as he sat up, his shaft hit different nerve endings and I released a loud moan. His mouth captured mine, his tongue invaded my mouth and danced with mine, devouring me, my whole body was heading towards an orgasm that would top the record books.

My body tightened and a fire bloomed in my core. It spread to my stomach and limbs until it reached my fingers and toes, as though pure pleasure was consuming me. It was almost painful in its intensity until Beast started moving. The friction of him moving out of me and back in caused the burning to twist itself, turning to ecstasy. A tsunami of exquisite bliss rolled and crashed against the fire in me, neither of them being diminished by the other, each wrecking me in their own way.

Orgasms had never felt that way with my vibrator. Even the ones Beast had given me with his mouth didn't compare...*nothing* had ever felt that way. I was soaring above my body, flying, and I had major doubts that I'd ever come back down.

I followed Beast. When he thrust, I rolled my hips into him. It felt right to my untrained body and the growls that he released let me know he liked it. With my body in turmoil, I desperately needed him to feel the same.

Beast wasn't just staring at me with glowing eyes, though. When he gritted his teeth and thrust into me harder, I noticed that his teeth had grown longer, sharper. The bare skin of his chest rippled between black and gold shimmers and his normal tanned flesh coloring. Gold veins ran through his skin. His shaft inside of me felt longer, harder.

It all just made me hotter. He wasn't in complete control of his body. Something was happening to him, just as it was happening to me. I gripped his shoulders and rode him, my body demanding more, demanding release. Harder, faster, I cried out and moaned his name while he hammered into me from below.

One of his massive hands came up and I saw that the tips of his fingers had lengthened into sharp claws. I should've panicked. I should've been afraid. Even as he gripped my hair and pulled my head to the side, I rode him. Even as he leaned forward and those sharp teeth flashed as he opened his mouth, I rode him. When those teeth sank into the flesh of my shoulder, the fire in my body won. A mix of burning, intense pleasure and pain overtook me.

Every single nerve ending in my body reacted. Electrical impulses surged through me and I screamed as my orgasm began to shudder through me. It raced through my veins, feeding into my core that tightened like a vice around Beast's swelling erection, and into my shoulder where I could feel Beast sucking at me, tasting me. Feeling like I'd split into a million pieces, my body tightened in on itself until the waves came rushing through, dousing everything in a pulsing, throbbing sensation of pure ecstasy. I came like a freight train on top of Beast, milking his cock until he shot his seed into me, a wild roar ripping from him as he yanked his teeth out of my skin and fell back into the chair, my blood dripping from the corners of his lips.

I watched him through heavy lids as my orgasm continued.

13

SKY

I came and then I went, out like a light. I passed out on Beast's chest and didn't wake up until the smell of roasting meat tickled my nose. I didn't want to open my eyes. I was on a cloud. It *had* to be a cloud. Nothing else could feel so soft and luxurious.

"Hello, beautiful mate." Beast's low voice came from somewhere in the room and I couldn't help but finally open my eyes to find him.

Standing in the doorway to the room, he was backlit. The only light in the dark room spilled in from the living room behind Beast. He looked bigger, more demanding than ever. I could see that he was naked, the backlit silhouette of his hanging shaft blush-worthy.

"Do I pass inspection?" He sounded amused, lighter than I'd ever heard him.

I sat up, bringing the blanket with me, and bit my lip. "What time is it?"

"Late. The sun went down an hour ago."

I gasped. "The boys!"

He stalked into the room and knelt beside the bed, his hands finding the blanket and slowly pulling it down. "I took care of them."

When I gasped again, he chuckled. The sound was so low and gravely that my pulse raced and tingle shot through my veins.

"I did not mean that I ended them. I would not hurt the young males, mate. They're mine now, too." His finger trailed down my neck, over my shoulder. When my skin tingled there, he smiled. "It's rare for a dragon to find his mate. My brothers here are overjoyed for me and they are celebrating. Cezar is a very good dragon and is quite fond of younglings. He has welcomed the males to his castle. They are excited to stay with him and with your blessing, he would like for them to stay a few days longer. Cezar is very set on the ways of this world. He will take them to school and cook them nice meals and care for them in any way they require."

"Oh..." I stuttered. "Uh, y-yeah, sure. He has my, um, *blessing*. You're sure Nick and Casey are okay with it? And that I can trust this Cezar?"

"I would trust Cezar with my own life. And yes, the young males were very excited to stay with Cezar."

Nick and Casey were probably happy to have a man around for a while. I felt another pang of guilt in regards to my parenting abilities and the fact that I hadn't provided the boys with a male role model to help them transition into manhood.

"We have a few days with no interference to enjoy each other." He hummed low in his throat. "And I would like to spend every second with you and most of them in this bed."

"But, work...I have to go to work."

"If you insist on going, I will take you."

"Bax..."

"The young males took him to Cezar's house. I just wish I could see the dragon playing with that mutant."

I was still riding a wave of pleasure induced stupor and I just nodded. I'd be going to work, but we could hash out the details later. The rest of what he was saying didn't make much sense, either, but I couldn't take it apart all at one time. I needed to be out of bed and a few feet away from Beast first.

"You are perfect." He stood up suddenly and scooped me under my arms, lifting me to my feet in the bed like a child. Almost eye to eye with me, he shook his head and ran his fingers through my hair.

"I never thought I'd find my mate. Especially here, in this world. Humans, I wouldn't have thought they were made to handle us. But, here you are. Perfect. And I shall be so gentle with you. And I shall care for you with everything I possess. I promise."

My knees felt weak. *I* was weak. I had so many things I needed to process and think through, but instead, I was so caught up in his compliments and sweet words that I couldn't think straight. "There are other worlds?"

He grinned. "Of course. My world was ruled by dragons. Some of us were harsh. Some, like Cezar were not."

"And you?"

His grin diminished. "I liked power."

My stomach twisted and I cupped his cheek in my hand. "What happened? Why did you come here?"

"The dragon slayers."

"There are dragon slayers?"

"There are always dragon slayers, little one. In my world, they rose up and fought harder than we thought possible. We underestimated them. A grave error. They killed thousands of our brethren. We could have stayed and fought. That was my choice, and I believed we could've killed them all. Yet, as was pointed out, not without enduring many more casualties on our side. Cezar, always a peacekeeper and diplomat, found a way for us to leave, to spare losing any more of our race. We lived. The slayers lived. Everyone won, or so he said."

"Are there dragon slayers here?"

He held my waist and pulled me into him. "A different sort, it seems."

"What?" Feeling instantly panicked, I looked around like there might be one of the hunters standing behind me waiting to drive a sword through Beast's chest. Or a bullet. I was so out of my league.

"Calm, mate. I just meant to say..." He hesitated and then kissed me. "According to our history, every dragon has its slayer. For some, it's literal. A sword, dagger, or an arrow to the heart, killing us dead.

For others, it's just a thing we say. Swords and arrows aren't the only way to take a dragon's heart. Sometimes, a beautiful human female with soft curves and kisses that light fires in one's soul is enough to capture a fierce dragon's heart."

I licked my lips and swallowed. It felt comically loud. "You mean me?"

He nodded. "Slayed me the second I saw you."

"Beast..." I shook my head. I wasn't... I couldn't be that for him. "I don't know about all of this."

"I do. You do, too if you allow yourself. You feel the connection between us. I know you do. You saw me lose control. You saw me in that in between form and you didn't run screaming. You even allowed me to mark you, drink from you. We are connected inside and out, now."

My heart sped up and I probably would've collapsed on the bed if he hadn't lifted me into his arms. We brushed against one another, bare skin to bare skin, and it was almost enough to make me forget how alarming his statement was. Almost. Truth be told, I couldn't be any sort of slayer to him. My first responsibility lay elsewhere. I couldn't give the boys the life they needed if I was shacking up with a...a... *dragon from another world*! It wasn't fair of me to give up on trying to create the stable, normal life that I'd been trying to create for the past six years. Something I definitely couldn't do if I was with Beast.

He wasn't wrong, though. I did feel something. I had from the start, too. Otherwise, I would've called the cops pretty much right away. When he'd followed me home, I would have called the cops. When he'd burst into my bedroom, I would have called the cops. When he'd refused to leave my house and ended up sleeping on the couch, I would have called the cops. When he'd grown sharp ass teeth and sank them into me, well, I would have screamed and run off the dock, but then I would have called the cops. Instead, despite my fighting it, I had reacted in a completely irrational manner because of my insane attraction to him.

It was like some sort of magic spell had suddenly taken over my entire listless and utterly magicless life and enchanted it. I wanted more, but I couldn't remain in the magic. It wasn't real. I knew I had to go back to *normal*, but wondered, nevertheless if maybe there couldn't be some sort of compromise.

I hated to do it, but I had to…"This is going to sound terrible, Beast, but… I can give this thing between us a week max, no more. I feel those things for you, I do, but I need to have a *normal* life. A *stable* life. A life where dragons are things of fairytales and medieval folklore. A life where I work my boring little waitressing job in a boring little café in Lafourche Parish and raise my two nephews up to be good, kind, hardworking southern gentlemen.

"If you can't agree to a week, I understand and will walk away now. I don't want to, though. This whole thing is a first for me—a first in so many ways, and I want to prolong it for just a few more days."

He sat down with me on his lap and repositioned me so I was straddling him. "You are mine, Sky. Forever. Dragons mate for life, and it is a very, very long life."

I shivered. "I can't do forever."

"You will. I'm going to take forever." His low growl told me that he truly planned on it.

I rolled my eyes. "Just tell me that you'll accept a week and then we'll figure it out." It was so selfish of me, but as much as I knew I should walk away right then with all his "*forever*" talk, I just wanted a few more days with him. "Please."

He scowled. "I did not expect the first time you begged me would be for me to let you leave."

I smiled, seeing that that was all the give I was going to get from him. "Maybe I could do a little of the other kind of begging, if it'd make you feel better."

He sighed and pouted like a little boy. "It would."

I sank to the floor between his knees and rested my hands on his bare thighs. "I've never done this before."

Beast's eyes glowed and I felt some of his power flood my veins. "What are you doing?"

I waggled my eyebrows. "It's called a blow job."

"A blow job?"

I took him in my hands and nodded. "Maybe you have a different name for it where you come from."

14

BEAST

We did not have *blow jobs* in the old world. In an instant, I rejoiced that we had left the old, outdated world behind for a new world where mates took your cock into their mouths. I dismissed any prejudices I had left of the old world being better. The new world was where I belonged. Not only because of my mate, but...blow jobs.

I was still thinking about it the next day while I watched Sky run around the café taking food and drinks to people. After a wondrous night together, I wasn't sure how she was still moving with so much pep. I was an immortal dragon. I had the ability to replenish everything my body needed almost instantly but she was a human.

Her movements were slightly stiffer. Obviously, those last few rounds of love-making had left her sore. She'd driven me mad with desire, though. Her cries, demanding more each time, could not be ignored. No self-respecting dragon would deny his mate. It was my duty to satisfy my Sky. When she begged me to drive into her hard and fast, I'd worried about breaking her, but she'd taken me and given just as good.

My mate was perfect. Not just perfect for me, although she was that, but perfect—in every way. I watched the human males in the place carefully. Surely, they could all see how beautiful, how special, she was. I worried that they'd want to try to fuck her. I'd kill any of them that dared to touch her. She was mine. Despite her silly idea of a week, I'd never let her go. She wouldn't be able to leave me, either. She was marked. We were joined.

Soon, she would realize that she had no reason to want to leave me. I would tend to her every need. I would shower her with everything she wanted, and I would do the same for the young males. I would fight for them just as fiercely as I would fight for her because they, too, were our family. I needed only to wait until the realization sunk into her head that we were fated to be together and that our lives were interwoven forever.

She glanced over at me like she could hear what I was thinking, and rolled her eyes. It made me want to pull her down on the table and lick her cunt until she screamed. She knew that, too, since she grinned and swayed her hips as she walked away.

Fuck. Everything about her made me come alive. My home no longer felt lonely, and after the boys came home to stay with us, it would be even better. Or, if she wanted something different, I'd build her that. I didn't care. I'd build whatever castle she wanted, wherever she wanted.

She sashayed her plump ass over to me after a few minutes and stopped too far away from me. "You could just go home, you know?"

"And do what? Wish I was looking at you?"

Her cheeks turned red and she tucked some loose strands of hair behind her ears. "You could do whatever it was you did before me. Live your life."

"What life? Before you, I was waiting for you. I did nothing before you, little one. I've been here, in this world, for almost eighty years and all I've done is become relatively companionable with an alligator and build my castle."

Her eyes went wide. "Eighty years?"

"About."

"How old are you?"

I raised my eyebrows, like she did. "You don't ask a dragon how old he is."

"A hundred?"

I shook my head.

"Two hundred?"

Again, wrong.

"*Three* hundred?"

"Nope."

"What? You're older than three hundred?"

"A lot older."

She swayed and then leaned against the table. "Holy shit."

I shrugged. "I think I look good for my age."

She suddenly laughed, the bright tinkling sound of it drawing the attention of almost every male in the room, which was unfortunate, because although it made my cock harden, it also made me want to kill the other males who could hear it. "You look good for any age."

I puffed my chest out and raised my chin in pride. "When can we leave?"

She looked at her watch and licked her lips. "I have another four hours. I get a break in a little bit, though. We could maybe take a walk."

"I don't want to walk."

She leaned over and pressed her lips against my ear. From that angle, I could see straight down her shirt and her heavy breasts bounced slightly in front of me. "Unless you want to have a quickie right here, in front of everyone, we have to take a walk."

I growled. "I will allow no one to see you."

"Then we'll take a walk, my possessive dragon."

I kissed her hard, it was what I needed in that moment to calm myself. "Hurry."

She moved away, stopping by tables and charming people as I watched. She smiled sweetly and treated everyone as kindly and as friendly as possible and I watched as they naturally fell for her charms. It wasn't hard to imagine her in the old world, in my old castle, entertaining my people as she fed them. She was the perfect queen.

Then, she was grabbing my hand and pulling me out of the front door with her. Around the side of the building and behind an old rusted out truck that blocked us from view of anyone who happened to look down the alley towards us. And my queen dropped to her knees in front of me and took my cock into her mouth. Before I spilled my seed, I dragged her up and pushed her over the back of the truck. Sliding into her tight sheath felt like coming home.

While I hadn't been sure about the idea initially, by the time we were finished and back inside the café, I was a fan of quickies. My head spun and she was in complete domination of every one of my senses. Her smell, her taste, the feel of her, it was all I could process. Watching her walk around, smiling politely, knowing that I'd just released my seed in her, it fueled a flame inside that I didn't know what to do about. I couldn't just throw her over my shoulder and take her home, but holding on to my sanity was a savage battle as everything about her pushed me towards doing just that.

I hoped she would not be able to walk away because if by chance she managed to, it would kill me. I would never be done. There was no way. I simply needed to show her why we belonged together, why it was the only thing that made sense.

15

SKY

I wasn't sure how I'd managed to make it through the entire work day without losing my mind. Even the quickie with Beast hadn't been enough. I was sore and exhausted, and still my body demanded him—craved him. I'd gone from a virgin to a raging nymphomaniac in less than a day. Nothing like making up for lost time.

After work, I was barely able to wait for him to fly us to his castle before I ripped off my clothes and we made love on the dock. The wood dug into my back and Beast had to find a splinter that had lodged itself in my hip, but it had been hot and so worth it.

Another round later in the shower, and I was dressed in one of Beast's shirts and a pair of his boxers that I'd had to roll about a hundred times to keep up on my hips. I was staring across the house at Beast as he worked on making something in the kitchen. I was contemplating whether or not I had it in me to go at it again right there in the kitchen. The muscles in my thighs were achy and my core was almost too sensitive to be touched, but he was so delicious and I wanted him again.

In just a pair of boxers, he moved through the kitchen, making something for us to eat. His back rippled with strength, his meaty ass and thick, strong thighs flexed as he grabbed something from the fridge making me drool. His hair was still wet from the shower. He was hotter than any man should ever be allowed to be. It was eating my brain to be so turned on by him constantly.

"Beast."

His back stiffened, but he didn't turn to face me. "Don't say my name like that when I know you're too sore for me to make love to you again right now, Sky."

I got up and strode across to him. Wrapping my arms around him and pressing my cheek against his back, I sighed. "What is happening to me? I can't stop this lustful ache to have you inside of me."

He held my arms and blew out a rough breath. "You'll be used to me eventually, little one, and you won't get as sore."

Eventually. That word. It soured my stomach. We didn't have eventually. No matter what he said.

I pulled away and settled on one of the stools at his island. "I want to check on the boys tonight."

He was quiet for a few minutes and then turned to look at me. "Cezar is bringing them over for you to see."

"How do you know?"

He tapped his head. "We can communicate. He'll be over soon. They're playing some game right now."

I tried to picture the boys playing a game. They never wanted to play with me. "Really?"

"Yeah. They're trying to teach him how to play a video game. He's as old as I am, though. Technology isn't our best skill."

I giggled at the image. "What do you all do during the day to keep busy? If you don't work, don't have girlfriends, and don't do technology, what *do* you do?"

Beast stared down at the oven and cursed. "We do the same things we did in the old world. As much as possible. I built this house. I updated it after fifty years or so. I read, though the books here are strange. I tried to learn to cook for myself, but stoves do not like me."

I bit my lip and grinned. "You cooked last night. It was good."

He shook his head. "Cezar made that and dropped it off while you were sleeping. He has a stove like the ones we had in the old world. Despite trying to humanize himself, he can't help some things."

"I could teach you."

He looked me over at me and then nodded. "Come over here."

The fluttering in my heart moved down to my stomach and then lower. I was mesmerized by the way his voice dropped. His words, like thick honey, tempted me. Even some of his bossiness was growing on me.

I moved over to the stove and peeked in the oven. The chicken he'd put in was charred. "Maybe you want to just cook it for a shorter duration."

His arms came down on either side of me and boxed me in. His large body rubbed against my backside and I felt his erection poking into my back. "Maybe I should hire a cook."

I swayed my hips into him. "Maybe. It might be difficult for you to fuck me over the kitchen counter if there was a cook here, though."

He growled and buried his face in the crook of my neck. His teeth raked over the mark on my shoulder that wasn't fading and one of his hands dropped to the front of my shorts and pressed against my mound. "Is that what you want, Sky? Do you want me to fuck you?"

Every hair on my body stood up and I panted. "Yes. I want you to fuck me hard and fast and don't hold back. I'm not as fragile as you seem to think."

"I don't know if you can handle it, little one. I don't want to hurt you. I've made love to you and treated you like my queen, because you are. Do you think you can take me all-out fucking you?"

My core dripped and my body weakened like someone had pulled a magic trick with my bones. Everything felt like jelly. "Tell me how it would be."

"Rough. Me fucking you would be rough, Sky. I'd fuck you so hard that you screamed for me. I'd spank that plump, delicious ass of yours and pull your hair. I'd use you however I wanted. If I wanted to pull out of your sweet pussy and slide into this beautiful ass, I would. I'd tie you up and use you until I'd come all over you and you begged

Fire Breathing Beast 77

me to stop so you could rest." He nipped my neck. "I wouldn't stop, though. Not until I'd had my fill."

I panted. My core constricted, practically begging for him to thrust into me. "Beast…"

"Is that something you want, little one? You want to be fucked like one of the castle whores?"

Time froze as the words settled around us. I couldn't tell which one of us stiffened first. I escaped from under his arm and turned to glare at him. "You had castle *whores*?"

His grimace said it all. He wanted to take the words back, but it was too late. They were echoing in my head, loud and clear. "That was a long time ago, Sky. Another lifetime."

"That's how you fucked them, though? You fucked them rough and hard and you yanked their hair? Is that right? Jesus, Beast."

"I don't fuck you like that, Sky. I make love to you. You have nothing to be angry about."

I pointed at him. "I felt you hard against me when you were talking about it. You want to fuck me like that. You want to reminisce about how you used to spend time with your castle whores? Who the hell are you? *Castle whores*?"

"I was hard because *you* make me hard. If I want to fuck anyone, it is *only* you."

"Do you have women like that here? Whores you fuck? Do you think you're going to have me and them, too?"

"No!" The roar he let out shook the house, yet I refused to flinch. "I will never want anyone but you. What don't you understand about mates?"

"Any of it! I don't understand any of it." I marched over to the living room and dropped into one of the couches. I felt angry and hurt. And completely irrational. It didn't make any sense for me to be acting like that. Yes, I knew it. I was jealous, though. I was jealous of a life he'd led so long before he'd met me that I hadn't even been born yet. "I don't understand anything about mates, Beast."

He knelt in front of me. "Now that I have found you, you are the only female I will ever desire. I would never touch another. I couldn't.

The thought of it makes me ill. I would not even be able to get hard for any other female. The idea of fucking you is what made me hard, not some faded memories from two hundred years ago. I'm sorry I said something that upset you."

"I'm sorry you said it, too." I crossed my arms and sniffled as tears threatened to fall.

"Please, Sky. Forgive me. We are mates. There will never be anyone else for either of us. I will never look at another female. You should never look at another man, not if you want him to remain living."

I rolled my eyes feeling incredibly, pitifully ridiculous, but I said it anyway. "This is only for the week, remember."

16
BEAST

I was a complete moron for saying that to Sky. In my defense, I wasn't used to being around females. I forgot that with females a dragon had to watch his tongue. Males either didn't get upset when you said something you didn't mean and went on to correct yourself, or we brawled, beat on each other, and then it was over. I cursed myself for being stupid enough to say something like that to her. She was nothing like a castle whore. I would never see her that way no matter how rough and dirty our lovemaking became. She would always be my queen. I wanted to roar a flaming, fiery inferno, though, for her sticking with the silly notion of us only lasting a week. Even though I knew it couldn't be cut short, ever, it hurt to hear her say that.

"It's not just for a week. You're lying to yourself if you really think that."

She frowned. "Beast... I have a life to get back to."

"A life that includes me, now."

"No. You're...great. You're a *dragon*, though, Beast. I live a normal life, in a normal world and that's how I like it. I have to go back to it. This is fun and exciting; it has been the thrill of a lifetime for me and

I promise you I will never forget it, but I can't exist in your world. The boys can't, either."

The tension in the room was high and hearing her use my being a dragon as an excuse to leave made me angry. I stood up and moved to the other side of the living room. "You can't be with me because I'm a dragon?"

She nodded. "Yes. I'm just a regular, everyday human. My boys are regular, everyday humans. You're hundreds of years old. Thousands maybe. You live in the middle of a swamp. I'm just this woman who's going to grow old and die in fifty or sixty years. You and I just don't mesh. We come from different worlds. Literally."

"That's bullshit. You're not a *regular* human. You're the mate of a warrior dragon. And we do mesh. Very well. We were meant for each other. What don't you understand?"

"And if I don't want to be meant for you?" The words were so quiet that I could almost pretend that I'd imagined them. Almost. "What if I *want* to be a normal human and go back to the way things were? What if all of this is too much for me?"

"I do not believe you. You are no coward." My voice shook, anger threatening to throw me into an uncontrolled shift. "You would not run from this because you are frightened of it."

The tears that had been glistening in her eyes finally fell. She turned her head and wiped them away. "You don't know that. You don't know me."

The faraway sound of Cezar's wings alerted me to his presence. I growled. "Cezar and the young males have arrived."

She jumped up and ran her shaking hands through her hair. "Maybe the boys and I should go…"

I stilled, not able to process that she was really going to try and leave me. "You promised a week."

"It'll just hurt more, Beast."

"I don't care. I get a week."

She nodded. "Fine. A week."

"I am going to change your mind." I grabbed her around the waist and pulled her into me for a punishing kiss. When I pulled away, I could hear the three males tromping up the dock. I growled against her lips and cupped her sex. "You are mine, Sky. You always were and you always will be."

She pulled away from me and I released her just before the knock at the door. She was flushed and I scented her sweet arousal. I didn't understand why she chose to fight this so hard, but it would work out. I hoped. It had to.

I opened the door and the young males rushed in, both of them wide-eyed and practically bouncing. Looking past them, at Cezar, I nodded a welcome to him. "I take it they liked the flight?"

He grinned. "Yeah, I'd say."

"Sky! We flew here! *Flew*!" Casey threw his hands in the air and he looked nothing like the tormented male he had been.

Even Nick, the older and more mature male, was giddy with excitement. "Legit. We flew. On the back of a dragon. A real dragon!"

She gave them a sneaky look and grinned. "How do you think Beast brought me here after work?"

Casey gasped and brushed his hair back from his face. Holding his forehead, he shook his head. "This is cray cray. What does Beast's dragon look like? Cezar's is bright green!"

"With streaks of gold." Nick tossed a look over at Cezar and smiled. "That's the real show."

I felt a pang of jealousy. Nick belonged to me. He and Casey came with Sky and she was definitely mine. I wasn't pleased that he was more impressed with Cezar than with me, but I would change that. "Are you ready to see your second dragon of the night?"

Casey's eyes went even wider. "Yes!"

Nick nodded, too, looking even more thrilled. "That'd be sick!"

Cezar tossed me a disbelieving look, but I ignored him. I could impress the young males, too. We all went outside and I kept my back to them while I stripped out of my boxers and then made a big show of running down the dock and leaping into the air.

I shifted in midair and by the time I was descending towards the water, I had already extended my wings and was pumping, elevating my body up towards the darkening sky. I threw my head back, made sure I was clear of the trees, and let out a big breath of fire before diving back down towards the water.

Nick and Casey were cheering at the end of the dock, but Sky was still on the patio, her arms crossed over her chest. She was pretending to be blasé and to anyone else, she may have looked the part. I knew better, though. Even as high up as I was, I could tell she was dazzled by me. Her body radiated desire. I scented it.

Cezar must certainly have been able to scent her too if I could, and he was too fucking close. I breathed a rain of fire that he had to leap to his left to avoid. Roaring, I swooped down and grabbed Sky.

She let out a startled shriek, but, like she'd been doing it her whole life, easily grabbed my neck and swung herself around so she was riding the back of my neck. Letting out a wild laugh, she leaned back and I glanced over my shoulder to see her hair flying in the wind and her arms lifted. I could hear her heart racing and smell her. She was so aroused, I almost felt her dampness against my scales.

I flew down and hovered above the lake letting Sky say goodnight to the males. We had somewhere else to be.

She called to them. "Are they okay with you for another night, Cezar?"

I growled at hearing her say his name, but her calming hand on my neck quieted me.

"They're great. We're having a blast. We're going to go learn more about the Call of Duty game together."

"It's so awesome, Sky! Cezar makes us strap in with something he made so we could ride him. *Safely.*" Casey bounced on his feet and fist pumped the air. He was obviously almost too excited to handle what was happening.

"Hey. If you fell off and broke your neck, your aunt wouldn't like me very much, would she?"

"Yeah, yeah, I get it." Casey closed the gap between himself and Cezar and gestured excitedly at us in the air. "Let's fly together."

After some encouraging from the young males, Sky and Cezar agreed and then we were all soaring through the night sky together. High enough that we wouldn't be seen, but low enough that they could get an unobstructed view of Lafourche Parish. I allowed it until I could feel Sky wiggling on my back, eager to be alone with me.

I signaled to Cezar that we were out of there and Sky called her goodbyes to her young nephews. When they shouted back that they loved her, too, I felt her heart skip a beat and then she hugged my neck tighter and sighed happily. How could she think leaving me would be better for her and them? No human male could give them what I could. No human male could have the young males shouting like toddlers into the night air as their dragons dove towards the earth. No human male could pleasure her until she screamed.

Only I could do that. No one would worship her like I did.

17

SKY

Flying through the night sky at what felt like a hundred miles per hour, I laughed into Beast's neck. The gulf was below us and it was the wildest thing, knowing that in a matter of minutes, Beast had flown me to the ocean. The stars shown overhead like millions of sparking diamonds, with no light that far out to distract from them. Everything about the night felt like some stolen adventure that belonged to some fairytale princess, or at least someone much less *normal* and *regular* than me.

My body pulsed against Beast's. Something about him shifting turned my blood to fire and all I wanted to do was feel him inside of me easing the ache between my thighs. Some carnal hunger spiked in me until I was helplessly forced to surrender to it. It didn't matter if I was sore or tired. I needed him to quench my longing.

"Beast, where are we going?" I didn't think I could stand waiting much longer.

He dove low and dipped his claws into the water, splashing it up at us. The chilled water did nothing to cool my overheated libido. He changed directions and a few seconds later, he dipped low again. That time, he descended on a strip of land that I hadn't been able to see.

Not much bigger than my backyard, the tiny island held nothing more than sand and a lone piece of driftwood. Until Beast shifted back, his dragon took up practically the entire space. Under the moon, I could just make out enough to know what was around me. Beast shifted and then the man was in front of me, his eyes glowing and his face a contrast of shadows and moon glow.

"What is this place?"

He grabbed the hem of the shirt I wore and yanked it over my head. "It's an island. We did not have these in my world. Like your blow jobs, they're a wondrous addition to this new world that I greatly appreciate."

My core fluttered and I shoved the boxers down my thighs. Stepping out of them, I closed the distance between us and pressed my body against his. His chest hair teased my nipples causing me to moan at the sensation of his erection trapped between us.

"Are you going to make love to me, or are you going to fuck me?" I couldn't help teasing him.

"Tell me, little one, what *you* want. Do you want me to make love to you?" He leaned down and trailed his tongue along my throat. "Or do you want me to fuck you?"

Lava. I was lava encased in nerve endings. I felt alive with so much power coursing through my body that I thought I might instantaneously combust. Under the moon, in the wide open, the ocean lapping at the sand a few feet away, I wanted everything from him. When I walked away, I wanted no regrets, nothing left undone.

"Fuck me."

Beast

I would've done anything for Sky. She was my world. My one true mate for life. Being asked to fuck her was hardly a chore. I didn't want to hurt her, though and losing all control with her could do just that.

She was small and soft and delicate and perfect. I was none of those things.

"I want you to fuck me, Beast. I want to feel you, all of you, without any holding back She stroked her hands up my chest and moaned. "Please."

"Are you begging me, little one?" My cock hardened even more, so much it hurt.

She dropped to her knees in the sand and stared up at me through those long eyelashes. Her eyes held mine as her tongue stroked over her lips. "Does it make you harder to know that I would beg?"

I cursed. "Yes."

That pink tongue flicked out again and she licked the tip of my cock. Then, she opened her mouth and took in nearly half of my length, closing her lips over my shaft and sucking hard as she pulled off. "Please, Beast. I need you. I need you to fuck me and use me however you want. Pleeease. Make me scream for you."

I felt more beast than man in that moment. Hearing those words from her sweet lips and feeling her tongue stroking the underside of my cock, was like being tortured by exquisite pleasure. My body coiled up with the need to fuck her rough and hard, but my mind told me to be easy. I would die if I hurt my mate.

She must have seen my hesitation, my slight reluctance. "If you won't fuck me, maybe there's another big dragon out there that will..." Her teasing voice was followed by a deep suck, but then she squealed, her teeth raking against my cock, as I hauled her up and pushed her over the big piece of sun bleached drift wood.

I grabbed the hair on the back of her head and pulled her head up as I dug my cock against her crack. I scraped my teeth up her neck and then held the front of her throat in my hand and whispered gruffly against her ear. "I don't like that joke, little one."

She arched her back and rolled her hips, trailing my pre-cum over the plump flesh of her ass. "Begging wasn't working fast enough, and I need...I need—"

"This?" I found her core dripping wet and thrust my cock into her fully in one sharp movement. "Or this?" I flicked my thumb over her little bundle of nerves.

She cried out, her small hand grasping at the hand I still held over her throat. Her nails bit into my skin as her tight little pussy squeezed me hard. "Beast! Yes!"

I pulled all the way out and sucked hard on her shoulder. "Like this, Sky?"

She arched her back even more, trying to get me back into her, but I stayed just out of reach. "You want me to say it again? You didn't like the joke, but I don't like being teased. If you can't do it, I'll find another dragon. Maybe Cezar?"

I rammed into her so hard that she would've been dumped on the other side of the log had it not been for my hand holding her throat. The beast in me wanted her to know that I was in charge. I was the boss, the one who made the rules and I pounded her with a thunderous frenzy. Her bouncing breasts were riveting. I dropped my hands to them and held them, squeezing the tantalizing flesh while I continued the brutal pace.

Sky screamed my name and clawed at my arms while I fucked her brutally. Her core pulsed around me hard and fast, like her body couldn't catch up to what was happening. When I raised one of my hands and slapped her on the ass, she reached back and tugged at my hair. "Yes, don't stop. Don't fucking stop."

I growled in her ear as I thrust in and out of her. Pulling almost all the way out and then ramming back in, I felt myself bottoming out in her, touching the depths of her. I wanted to spill my seed there, mark the deepest recesses of her as mine. "I'm going to come in you, Sky. I'm going to release my seed deep in you. You are mine. You will never be with anyone else. I won't let it happen."

Her body tightened, squeezing me so hard it was almost painful. Her hand in my hair yanked harder. "I'm going to come, Beast." I stopped.

"Not until you tell me that you're mine." I rammed into her once and withdrew, my hand raining more slaps on her ass. Her skin was bright red and I loved the look of my handprint on her pale ass. I wanted my marks to be everywhere.

"Beast!" She hung her head, but I held her throat again and forced her head up. Looking at me over her shoulder, she bit her lip, struggling with what to do.

"Tell me that you're mine, Sky." I pumped into her once, very slowly, and again withdrew and waited.

Her lips stayed closed, but I could see the neediness in her eyes, begging me to let her come. One more slap on her ass.

"Say the words." I dropped my hand to her bud and lightly tapped just above it. "Say them and I'll let you come."

"I'm yours!" Her scream only went higher when I thrust into her and circled her bud before pressing down on it. Her orgasm shattered me and I came hard with her, sinking my teeth into her shoulder, marking her again and again.

"*Mine.*"

18

SKY

I woke up the next morning in Beast's cloud bed, unsure of how I'd gotten there. I felt like I'd been run over, but as I stretched, there was a warm pleasantness to the aches that made me smile. I looked over at the clock and groaned. I had to get to work.

I could hear Beast in the shower, humming some old fashioned sounding song that I didn't quite recognize. I wanted to join him, but I knew what would happen and my body couldn't handle it. Instead, I slipped out of the room and into the guest bathroom. I took a record short shower and dried off while staring at my body in the mirror.

I was covered in bruises. My hips were bruised from Beast's fingers digging into me. My thighs had bite mark shaped bruises, along with my neck and shoulders. My ass was still an irate shade of pink from his slaps. My thighs had finger shaped bruises, too.

I swallowed and wrapped the towel tightly around me. Something about the bruises scared me. My normal, boring life was slipping away. They didn't hurt, the opposite actually. Looking at them turned me on. I wanted more of the sex that had left them. Even the rough sex from the night before... I wanted it all. That wasn't me, though. At least, I didn't think so. The night before was a woman who was obsessed with getting as much of a man as she possibly could. She was hungry for him. I wasn't her.

I couldn't lead a normal life covered in bruises from fucking like an animal with a dragon. I'd have to make sure no one saw the marks and assumed that I was some kind of kinky sex enthusiast. I wasn't. Okay, maybe I was, but just with Beast.

"Hey. What are you doing in here?" Speaking of the man, he stood in the doorway, wearing low slung jeans and looking like the cover of a romance novel.

"I didn't want to start anything. I'm feeling a little sore."

He came over and stood behind me, his eyes trailing over me in the mirror. "Are you okay?"

I could hear the remorse in his voice and I hated it. I turned to face him and nodded. "I'm fine. Just sore. It was...*good*. You know that."

He forced a smile. "I was too rough, though. I should've held back more. I should've—"

"Should've nothing. You did exactly what I asked you to."

"I can feel your mood. It doesn't feel okay."

"What do you mean?"

"We're mates. You are marked as mine. We're synced, now. For life. Eventually, soon maybe, we'll be able to communicate to each other through our minds, when I'm in my dragon form, especially. I can already feel some of your emotions. They aren't good right now."

I stepped back. "What?"

"You're wet for me, like you always are, but you're sad." He sighed. "You're still thinking that you can walk away."

"What do you mean, Beast? You can read my mind? What the fuck?" I ran my hands through my wet hair and shook my head. "This is all too much."

"I can't read your mind, yet. I can just read your emotions, Sky. It's a built in response to mating. It helps me cater to your needs so I can always keep you happy."

"Too fucking much." I stepped away from him. "I have to get ready for work."

"We'll talk about this later, then." A command, instead of a request.

I kept my mouth shut and went to find my work clothes. I just needed to get to work and clear my head. I could zone out while serving and maybe sneak in a talk with Amie. I needed time to figure out what to do about Beast. I needed time to make up my own mind, instead of having him tell me what was going to happen.

Things progressively went downhill, though. As if sensing my pulling back, Beast was even more bossy than usual. He was cranky, too, and I didn't need to be able to read his mind to know that.

At the café, he sulked in his booth and picked at his three plates of pancakes. Beast never picked at food. He watched me with a dark look on his face and I could tell that we were in for a doozy of a fight. He wanted things the way he wanted them and I wasn't going to give in to him. Certainly not because he pointed and demanded. Not because he *told* me that we were mates.

Amie was through the roof happy because she'd gotten great news about her prospects of having a baby, so she stayed away from our darkness. I didn't blame her.

When my tips suffered and I started getting snide remarks from customers, my mood soured even more. Having at least a tiny bit of space away from Beast gave me the ability to think, and think I did. I was furious. He was being a controlling asshole and he had been from the start. I'd just been too blinded by lust to care.

I didn't want that, though. I didn't want him following me to work and telling me what I could or couldn't do. It didn't matter that the sex was explosive or that I actually liked him when he was being calm with me. Between his attitude and the fact that I existed in the very real world, where magic was for kids' birthday parties and TV shows, it just didn't make sense to continue with him. No matter what he said about mates, we obviously weren't meant to be.

Why did admitting that feel like a sledgehammer had landed on my chest. I'd only known him for a few days for goodness sakes. I'd be fine.

I was feeling darker than ever when a hand snaked out from a table I was passing and pulled me to a stop. I glared down at the hand and then into the face of a man I didn't know.

"Whoa, calm down, sweetheart. I just wanted to talk for a second. You look like you could use some cheering up." He talked to my chest and grinned like a slime ball. "Can I buy you a coffee?"

I shook my head. "No, thanks. I'm working."

"How 'bout a drink later, then?" He winked and shrugged. "I'm sure you could use a little something to relax after a long day. Maybe a shoulder massage?"

I was about to tell him how much I didn't need drink or a shoulder massage if they were coming from him when a big arm wrapped around my waist and pulled me away. Looking back, I saw Beast glaring down at the man.

"Touch her again and I'll rip your fucking arms off."

Beast's deep, ominous threat drew the attention of the entire café and I felt my face burn bright red. I grabbed his arm and tried to pull him away.

"Dude, chill out. I just asked her out for a drink. If she didn't want to go, all she had to do was say no."

"She's *mine*. You touch her or talk to her like that again and you will not have to worry about anyone saying no ever again. There will be nothing left of you to say no to."

In response to the sudden hush that had descended over the café, Marcus emerged from the back. He took in the situation with a scowl. Marching over to us, he looked from me to Beast and pointed to the door. "Out. This isn't happening in here."

"Marcus, I'm sorry. It won't happen again. I just—"

"Out, Sky. Don't come back until you get this sorted out. This doesn't fly here. You know that." He looked at Beast and jerked his arm towards the door again. "Did you hear me? I said get out."

Beast growled at him, too. He was on the verge of losing control and I pulled him as hard as I could. He finally wrapped an arm around me and stalked towards the door. "You're better than this place, anyway."

Amie appeared at the door with my purse and a frown on her face. "Call me, Sky."

I just nodded, angry tears threatening to fall if I opened my mouth to speak. Leaving the café, I knew what had to be done.

19

BEAST

Furious didn't begin to describe what I was feeling. Murderous was closer. The human male got off easy. My blood boiled and I wanted to go back into the café and rip the puny loser's limbs from his torso. At least Sky didn't have to return there anymore. She was free to stay at home and spend her time with me.

"Fucking asshole. Thinking he can just touch you and make advances on you. You are mine. He is lucky to be breathing." I shook my head.

Sky didn't say much and I could feel that she was angry, but I assumed her anger was directed at the man in the café. I shifted and she climbed on like always. I felt her heartrate increase and smelled her arousal, but she didn't cling to me like she normally did. She felt cold and removed.

By the time we landed at my house, I'd figured out that she was angry with *me*. When I shifted back, she pushed away from me and stormed into the house.

"What are you doing?"

She grabbed the few things that she had in my room and then stormed back outside. "I'm going home."

"What?"

She stormed down the dock and tossed her things in her boat that was still tied up where the young males had left it that first night. "I'm not doing this with you."

I laughed. "This? Sky, come inside and we'll talk."

"No. I'm going home. You're not going to snap your fingers and command me inside like I'm a dog." She climbed into the boat and went to untie it, but I grabbed the rope.

"What is wrong with you, mate?"

"You're a controlling, self-centered asshole. You're bossy. You're pushy. And you're condescending! I'm done." She glared at me. "You've done nothing but boss me around. You tell me how it is and how it's going to be. You didn't even stop to explain to me what being a mate meant or what would happen, or why it was special. You just came up, demanding that I was yours and that it was fucking great. Well, I'm on the other side and it's not great!

"You may have just cost me my job. It may be nothing to you, oh high and mighty one, but it meant a whole lot to me. I don't have a degree, I don't have any other useful skills. I waitress. That's what I'm good at and that's how I make money to take care of myself and the boys. You just showed your ass in there, for nothing, and threw a huge wrench into my life.

"I don't need any more difficulties. Things are challenging enough for me right now. This is one straw too many. I'm not cut out for this. I just want a normal life, Beast. A normal life where the man I'm with talks to me and we have conversations. He doesn't just bark orders and expect me to follow them. You just tell me to jump and are shocked when I don't ask how high. That's not a relationship. This isn't a relationship."

I yanked the rope tighter and growled. "Stop it, Sky. This is a relationship. So, I am bossy. I take charge. It is my way. I'm not used to everyone talking and coming to decisions together. Your mate is an old school fucking dragon. You have to deal with it."

"That's where you're wrong." She yanked a knife out from under the seat of her boat and sawed at the rope, quickly cutting it in two. "I don't have to deal with it. I'm done. If you think that you don't have to change because you're a little older than me—okay, hundreds of years—and because you're a dragon, that's fine. You can stay right here and not change all by yourself. I don't want to be with a dragon, anyway."

I threw the damned rope down. "You cannot be done with me, Sky! We are mates! You carry my mark! The moment I sank my teeth into you, you became mine. You are tied to me. You will not age, you will not change. Our lives are directly linked now."

She stopped working the motor of the boat and jerked around to face me. "What did you say?"

"We are linked. Just like I can feel your emotions, I will always be able to find you. I will always be tied to you. You bear my mark." I swallowed, seeing her anger bubble up. "And you will not age, not as long as I'm still alive."

"Another choice you made for me."

"Of course, I made it for you! It is my duty. It is my duty to take charge and care for you."

"And make the decisions you thought were best for me."

"Yes! I know what you need. You need me. That's how it works."

"Oh, fuck you. It's not how it works for me." She turned her back to me and started the engine. "Forever is going to be a long time for us both, if what you say is true, Beast."

"Sky!"

"Tell Cezar to bring my boys home. We're done with this. It's time we got back to our lives. It's time I went back to living in the world of reality."

"You can't just walk away."

"You can't just make up your mind and decide for me what I need. You should try a conversation next time, Beast. It might work better for you."

"Sky, come on! Come back here!"

"Don't come to my house. I don't want to see you."

I roared angrily as she got farther away. "Sky!"

She tossed her hand up in a wave as her boat carried her farther and farther away.

I desperately wanted to chase her and drag her back. I was angry and hurt. She just walked out as though our mating didn't matter. What the hell was wrong with her? Because she was a human, did she not feel the mate bond like I did?

I stomped back up to my house and slammed the door closed. When that didn't make me feel any better, I yanked it open and slammed it again and again. Eventually, I ripped the heavy metal from the wall and threw it into the swamp. Still didn't feel better.

How could she say those things to me? How could she leave?

I told myself that if she did not want me, I was not going to beg her. I was a king among men. I did not grovel and beg on my belly like a starving mongrel. Even as I thought the words, though, I knew that if it would bring her back to me, I would implore her by crawling on my hands and knees over broken glass.

I needed to get drunk on the spirits of the old world with a few males who understood our ways. I called out to the dragons to gather for a rare meeting.

We dragons were solitary creatures, only together because we were forced to be to survive. We still hoarded our treasure and were very suspicious of others stealing it, but I didn't have anything I cared about guarding anymore. Not after losing my most valuable, most precious treasure. I called them all over and instructed Armand to bring his strongest brew. I needed something hard to make me forget.

20

SKY

By the time I got home, Cezar was waiting for me near the dock with the kids. In some awful way seeing him there, without Beast around making sure he didn't look at me for too long, was painful. Maybe Beast would come to his senses and realize that I was just a fun romp in the hay and then move on. That we weren't meant to be together forever, that he was mistaken. He'd simply been crazy with lust. Why that hurt me, I didn't know. Or like.

"What's wrong, Sky?" Nick asked as soon as I pulled the boat up next to the dock. "You're crying."

I reached up and touched my face. Hell, I *was* crying. I wiped at the tears angrily and shook my head. "I'm okay. It's nothing."

Casey reached for the rope to tie the boat up and frowned when he realized it wasn't there. "What happened to the rope?"

"I have to get going." Cezar nodded at me and smiled at the boys. "Come see me, guys. You can help with me with computer."

Casey groaned. "You need more than help."

Nick focused on giving me a hand out of the boat before we both dragged it onto the shore. "We already put Bax inside."

A memory popped into my head of when I awoke from a deep sleep to Beast's shouting about Bax on his chest and asking me what kind of creature the cat was. More of the stupid tears fell. God, I felt like a mush-face. I rounded on Cezar. "Don't you dare tell Beast that I was crying."

"I must. You're his mate. If I didn't, he'd have every right to knock my teeth out."

I scowled at him. "What makes you think I won't knock your teeth out?"

Casey laughed and grabbed my hand. "Come on, Aunt Sky. You can't beat up a dragon. Don't embarrass yourself."

"I'm going to see him now." Cezar shrugged. "You two need to work this out."

I gave him one last scowl before marching towards the house. I found Bax on the kitchen counter and scooped him into my arms before going to my bedroom and climbing into bed. Spooning the big, mangy cat against my chest, I let myself really bawl.

"Aunt Sky...what's wrong?" Nick came into the room and sat on the edge of the bed. "What happened with Beast?"

Casey came in and sat at the foot of the bed. "Why'd you leave there early? We thought you were going to be there for good. We were going to get our stuff ready to move in soon."

I sat up. "What?'"

"Yeah. Cezar told us all about how you're mates and that you're going to be together forever. That's how mates work. Why are you back here?"

I just stared at them. I thought I'd escaped talk of dragons and mates, but I should've known better. The boys were eager and excited with their new found magical world. "It's difficult."

Casey sighed. "Come on, Sky. How difficult can it be? We're poor. Beast is rich. He's a dragon. He can take care of us in more ways than just with money. Did I mention he's a freaking dragon? Plus, he can fly and once he lets up on that tough guy image, he's pretty cool."

Nick frowned. "I thought you liked him."

I stared at Casey. "It's about more than being rich or poor. Or that he's a dragon. Life doesn't work that way."

"It could. You're just making it difficult. Why do you do this? You could just let us be happy. We like him. We like Cezar. Why do you have to ruin everything?"

I sat up straighter and felt my back stiffen. I knew I was still crying, but I didn't care. "Stop it. I do everything I can to take care of you and make sure you have everything you need. You're acting like a spoiled brat. I'm sorry you don't get to be rich and live with a dragon, but that's just the way it is."

"I'm a spoiled brat? You're a selfish bitch."

The urge to slap him rose right up to the surface in me, but I remained in control of myself. We'd had enough violence in our family. I sucked in a deep breath and blew it out slowly. "Go to your room."

"No. You can't make me!"

Nick stood up and grabbed Casey by the collar of his shirt. "Just go! Why are you like this? Just go to your room and stop acting like a little asshole! Can't you see that she's upset? All you think about it yourself and I'm sick of it! We're all sick of it!"

Casey stumbled backwards and then swung at Nick. I jumped up from the bed and grabbed him. Walking him out of the room while he screamed and fought to get away, I held on, even as his wild punches and kicks landed on me.

Nick followed us, screaming back at Casey. "You're terrible! I always go along with you, but I'm done! You make everyone think that I'm the bad one, but I just want to be here and be quiet. I just want to live in one place! *You're* going to ruin everything, not Sky. You're going to make her hate us. She's going to go away, too. She's going to leave us, just like everyone else, and it's all going to be your fault!"

Casey screamed louder. "She'll leave anyway! Why can't you see that? She'll leave, too! We're always going to be alone!"

I shook him, harder than I probably needed to, my own anger and helplessness coming out in it. "Stop it! Fucking stop it! Both of you!"

When they were both still and quiet, I pushed Casey down on the couch and marched around in front of them. "I am done with this.

I'm done. I'm the adult, and I'm not leaving! I'm here. I'm here for both of you and I'm never going anywhere, and I'm never going to hate you. If you both keep this up, though, I am going to lose my mind and then you're going to be stuck with a lunatic as your aunt.

"Casey, you have to stop. You have to stop acting out and treating everyone around you like they don't matter. We're the only family you have here and you need to stop pushing us away. We're not going anywhere. We'll keep taking your abuse, but why do you want to put us through that? We love you. Just let us love you and stop hurting us."

Nick cried from next to me. "I don't want to fight. I hate the fighting. I hate it. Dad screamed and fought all the time. I don't want to be like him."

Casey's sobs wracked his small body. He curled in on himself and buried his face in his knees. Nick went to him and wrapped his arm around his little brother, holding him while they both cried.

I knelt in front of them, crying just as hard as Casey. I was exhausted. My heart hurt. I was trying to convince the boys that everything was going to be okay, while I felt like everything was falling apart. It wasn't okay. I had to put up a brave front for them, though.

I wrapped my arms around them both and held them, repeating the message I needed them to hear. "I love you both. I'm not going anywhere."

When all the tears had been cried, the room turned silent and awkward. Nick pulled away first, sat back and used his shirt to wipe his eyes. Casey sat back and stared at the wall behind me. I sat back on my heels and let my head hang down. I didn't have anything left in me.

"Sorry." Casey still didn't look at me.

Nick sighed. "Me, too."

I ran my hands through my hair and sighed, too. "Me, too. We're stuck together, guys. We have to make it work. It doesn't have to be perfect, but we're family."

They both shrugged, but I hoped to god that maybe there was some kind of compromise we could all reach. We had to. I loved them both and I'd never give up on them.

21

BEAST

Flying while drunk was only slightly less dangerous than driving while drunk. I should've stayed home and bitched and moaned about everything to the other dragons, but they were hardly sympathetic. I had a mate. They didn't. It was getting closer to the eclipse and if they didn't find their mates soon, they would eventually lose their minds. I didn't have to worry about that. I just had to worry about convincing my mate we belonged together.

I flew too low and hit the swamp behind Sky's house harder than I meant to. It sent me flipping end over end through the water until I finally stopped rolling and sank to the bottom like a drunken rock. I came up, spitting and sputtering, as a man.

Growling at my clumsiness, I swam over to the dock and pulled myself up on it. I meant to get up right away and stalk over to Sky's door, but suddenly, the earth felt unsteady under me. I was drunker than I realized.

"Sky!" I bellowed her name out into the night sky and hoped that she'd come to me. I had things to say that she needed to hear. "Sky!"

The other dragons' words crowded my brain. They thought I was stupid. If Sky just needed me to be less bossy and commanding, then I should be less bossy and demanding. Cezar went on a rant about modern, human Earth women appreciating the right to make their own decisions with their lives. Armand told me how creepy I was for insisting that she was mine for life. I got earfuls of them telling me what a moron I was, how they'd do anything for a mate, how no matter what she needed, they'd provide it.

The thing was, I felt the same. Yet, somehow, I'd messed everything up. It sounded so simple. Just be less demanding. If I could pull that off, would she come back?

"Sky!"

After what felt like a million years, I could smell her coming nearer. I tilted my head back and saw her in a big T-shirt and nothing else. Maybe underwear. If she'd just come closer, I'd be able to tell, but everything was swaying.

"What are you doing here?" She crossed her arms over her chest and frowned at me. "Are you drunk? What's wrong with you?"

"Yes, I'm drunk. My mate left me." I sighed and let my head fall back onto the dock with a thud. The wood hurt, but I didn't care. "You're beautiful. So beautiful."

"Jesus, Beast. You're trashed. Why are you here?"

"You left me."

She sighed. "Yeah."

"It hurts."

"Yeah."

I blinked up at her. "I can change."

She bit her lip. "Come on, Beast. Go home."

"No." I realized what I'd done there and groaned. "I mean, *please, no.*"

"Go home, Beast."

"We must talk. Human women like talking, right? Can we talk?" I realized I was begging, and that was fine with me. I would do anything if it meant not losing her.

"If we do talk, it's not going to be like this. You're drunk and you're just saying what you think I want to hear. This isn't you, anyway. You don't beg. Go home." She saw that I was about to argue and held up her hand. "Give me some time and then maybe we'll talk. I'm not promising anything, Beast."

I forced myself to sit up and groaned as everything spun. "I will fly home. When this world stops spinning so fast."

"Son of a bitch." She ran her fingers through her hair and nodded. "Fine. Get up. Come on. You can sleep here—on the couch. You have to leave in the morning, though."

I reached for her and felt a shudder go through my body as her mere touch ignited flames of desire inside of me. "With the mutant cat?"

"Don't call him a mutant." She wrapped her arm around me. "But, sure. You can sleep with Bax."

Even when she wanted me to go away from her, she was sweet. That knowledge settled in my sloshing gut as I swayed. If I didn't fix this, I'd never be okay. She was perfect, sexy, kind, gentle, and wild enough to take me on. She had that stubborn streak, but I was beginning to think it was part of what made her so special. If she just went along with whatever I said, I'd probably be bored. Maybe.

"Cezar told me that human women like to hear their males say certain things." I looked over at her. "In our world, we didn't say those things. We knew that if we found our mate, certain things were understood. You didn't have to say them."

"Beast..."

"I...love you...Sky...forever." My voice broke and I cleared my throat and repeated myself. "I love you, forever, Sky. I would do anything for you. I would die for you. That's love, right? Knowing that I would give anything and everything for you. You mean that much to me."

Sky stopped walking and blew out a breath. "Stop talking, Beast."

"Yes, I will stop talking. That is probably best."

"Yeah."

I let her help me to her couch and then I settled onto it as well as I could. "I am old, Sky. I am brutish, I am stubborn and I learned my ways a long time ago, in a very different place. Cezar has been learning to be better all these years. He started out a better dragon than me, though. I was never good. I am going to try to be better for you, though."

I felt the mutant jump on my chest and sighed. "Cezar said something about teaching a dog tricks. He said I could change."

Sky laughed gently and pulled a blanket over me. "You can teach an old dog new tricks."

"I'm the old dog?"

She ran her fingers along my jaw. "I think that's what he meant, yeah."

I turned into her touch and then she was gone. I faded into sleep thinking about how I must learn new tricks.

22

SKY

I slept later than I'd meant to, but we'd all decided that we were spending the next day in bed, anyway. That was before Beast had woken me up in the middle of the night. I hurried out of bed and rushed into the living room, not sure of what I would find, not even sure of what I wanted to find.

Surprisingly, true to his word, Beast was gone. There was a very roughly scribbled note left behind, though.

Forever.

His words replayed in my head: *I love you, forever, Sky,* and I sank onto the couch. He loved me. At least, he thought he did. I clutched the note in my hand and groaned. It didn't make anything any easier. Just because he thought he loved me and thought he wanted to change didn't mean that he would change. He could continue to be just as demanding and bossy as ever. Besides, even if he did change, he'd still be a dragon. There was no possible way to have a normal, regular life with a dragon in it. There just wasn't. It was a fun novelty for a while, some of which left me with a feeling of euphoria, but those types of things weren't long lasting. Eventually, real life set in, work, bills, car repairs, the search for colleges for the boys. A person needed to make rational decisions about who to include into their lives. Didn't they?

I looked down at the note in my hand again. *Forever.* I wouldn't age. As long as he lived, I'd live. Forever was a long time.

Lightheaded, I bent forward lowering my head between my knees. Jesus. When you didn't age, forever was...forever. He was several hundred years old. I would be several hundred years old one day. In several hundred years. Oh, jeez, I'm losing my marbles.

"Sky?" Nick called my name as he came into the room. "What's wrong?"

I sat up and forced a smile. "Nothing. Everything is okay. I mean *great*. Everything is great."

"Really? Because I thought I heard Beast bellowing your name outside last night."

I groaned. "You hear too much."

"Yep. So, why isn't he still here? Where did he go?"

Casey stumbled into the room. "Where's Beast?"

"Is there anyone in this family who didn't hear Beast last night?"

The boys answered simultaneously. "No."

Nick laid his hand on my shoulder. "You aren't really going to leave him, are you? Come on, Aunt Sky. He's a great guy."

My pulse quickened. "Boys, the three of us have a lot of work to do on our family. I've been trying so hard to provide you both with something you've never had, a nice, normal, stable family. That definition doesn't include dragons."

Nick scoffed. "Are you breaking up with him because you think we have a chance at being normal without him? Seriously? Sky, all the rest of our family is either dead, addicted to drugs, or in prison. Our dad, your brother, is in prison for things that we don't even talk about. We're never going to be normal. If you're trying to make us fit that definition, you're fighting a losing battle."

"We could be normal." I looked between the two of them and saw their disbelieving looks. "Shit. Maybe not."

Casey shoved my shoulder playfully. "We're just not that kind of family."

I held his gaze and caught his hand. "But we are a family. Right, Casey?"

He pulled his hand away and made a face, but nodded. "Yeah. We are."

Nick groaned. "Yeah, we're a family. A weird one."

Casey piped up, "So, go get Beast back 'cause he fits right in with us."

"It's not that simple."

"Why not?"

"He's bossy!" I said it and then bit my lip. They were both staring at me like I'd lost my mind. "I don't want to be bossed around. I want to make my own decisions."

The boys looked at each other and Nick raised an eyebrow. "Okay?"

I stood up and picked up Bax. He smelled like Beast and before I could help myself, I buried my nose in his fur. "It's adult stuff, okay?"

Nick shrugged. "All I know is that you were happy with him. I never saw you smile so much as in the past few days."

"I'm happy with you guys, too." I was defensive, worried that they saw something that I didn't. I *was* happy with them. "And I smile!" I did. And to prove it, I flashed a huge smile at them. Maybe a slightly over exaggerated smile because both boys burst out laughing.

"Not in the same way. You're all mushy when you look at him. I've never seen you laugh like you did when you were flying on his back." After Nick said that, Casey and Nick exchanged looks and some unspoken communication seemed to pass between them.

"We know you love us, Aunt Sky, and you're trying. But, it makes us feel good to see you smile like that. It makes our family better when you're trying less and smiling more. Still weird, but better."

My eyes teared up. I was momentarily stunned speechless. When did my oldest nephew become so mature and so wise beyond his years?

Nick stood up and walked towards his bedroom. "I'm going back to sleep. I think you should get him back. We really like him. You don't have to worry about us if you leave, either. I'm going to make sure that we don't get into any trouble. Right, Casey?"

Casey scowled but shrugged. "Whatever."

I watched as they both walked back towards their rooms and my heart throbbed. I felt as though we'd turned over a new leaf. Like they trusted me more and I could trust them more, too.

I stood there holding Bax, smelling Beast, and trying to make sense of all the thoughts and emotions swirling around my head. Maybe, I just needed to talk to him. I'd just go over and we could talk and figure out where to go from there.

My mind made up, I headed back to my bedroom to shower and dress. I chose a light sundress and braided my hair to keep it from sticking to me in the heat, then hurried back out of my room.

Nick and Casey were standing in the hallway watching me with grins on their faces.

Nick laughed. "Good choice."

"I'm just going over to talk to him." Why I was defending myself to my teenage nephews, I wasn't sure.

"We're going to be rich." Casey high-fived Nick and then they both went back into their rooms.

"That's a snooty attitude and not a sure thing at all!"

"Yeah, yeah."

I rolled my eyes and hurried out to the boat. As I navigated through the thick, murky water, tall grass and cattails in the direction of Beast's house, I tried to remain calm and repeat to myself over and over that I just wanted to talk.

The closer I got, the more nervous I became. I started questioning myself. Was I doing the right thing? Was I thinking clearly?

When I had just about convinced myself that I needed to turn around and go back home, I heard a faint rustling and flapping sound above and looked up to see five massively giant dragons in the air above me.

"Holy shit."

Beast's black and gold dragon wasn't among them, and as I watched, slightly mesmerized, my boat continued forward. I was a little shaken, and quite frankly awestruck, by the sight I'd just witnessed. It was amazing, really. They moved through the air with such ease, no fear of being seen, yet their kind remained secret. I was curious about that.

When the swamp opened up in front of me, I saw Beast standing on the dock, waiting for me. He was in a pair of low slung jeans that hugged his muscular thighs and a faded T-shirt, stretched taught over his well-built chest and biceps. How he could look so mouth-wateringly handsome in something so simple, was baffling. But, it was too late to turn back after he saw me. I powered the boat over to him and stopped.

He looked down at me, smiling. "I'd ask if you want me to tie you off, but there's no rope, huh?"

I fought a grin. "Can't you just pick it up and put it somewhere? You're strong enough, right?" I winked.

He laughed lightly, his smile so easy and yet so devastating. "Of course."

I took the hand he held out for me, climbed onto the dock and turned to watch as he effortlessly picked up my boat and set it on the dock behind us.

"Shall we talk on the patio?"

I nodded. I didn't totally want to talk. I was so nervous, being that close to him, that all I wanted to do was push and shove my boat back into the water and power the hell out of there. What if we couldn't come to some sort of agreement about the thing between us? Even more frightening, what if we could? I wasn't sure which scared me more.

He pulled a chair closer to his ergonomic exterior patio lounger and recliner and sat down. "You look like you might want to run."

I nodded nervously. "Thinking about it."

23

SKY

"Well, if that is your wish, I will not stop you."

I swallowed. Was it awful of me to wish that he *would* stop me? I had to make up my mind. "I'm nervous. That's silly, isn't it? I mean, you've seen me naked. In lots of ways. And all sorts of positions."

He growled. "Maybe we shouldn't talk about that right now."

I laughed awkwardly. "Yeah, right."

Silence settled on us and I thought about leaving again. This type of awkwardness was a first for us. I hated it.

"I don't know what to say. Maybe I shouldn't have come."

"Say what you're thinking, Sky. I would like to know what you want from me so that I can provide it."

I played with the hem of my dress. "I talked to the boys last night. And this morning. They said that I'm happier with you."

Beast sat forward. "Are you?"

"I think so." I hurried on. "I mean, yes. I am. I don't like when you're being too controlling of me, though. Nothing changes that, Beast. I'm my own person. I want to work and I don't want you there constantly, hovering and watching me and attacking people who are rude to me or who touch me. I can handle myself in the café. I've done it for years. Also, I don't want you making decisions that affect my life without asking me. That's not how relationships work."

"I'm learning that."

"I... I feel strongly about you. I like what we have and what we do. I feel happy with you, that's true. I just... I can't be with you if you don't treat me like an equal."

Beast leaned even closer to me. "You are not my equal. You are better than me. You are so precious to me that I got carried away. The feeling of finding one's mate is intense for a dragon. It's all-consuming. The very thought of something happening to you and me not being there to protect you, well, it made me go a little crazy. I can do better though. I will try hard."

I scooted towards him. "Are you going to let me live my own life?"

He grimaced, but nodded. "I cannot promise that I will be perfect at first, only that I will try. I will not bother you at work, and I was wrong to jeopardize the job that you love."

"And you won't just make decisions for me without consulting me?"

"I will do everything I can to make you happy, Sky. Whatever it is you need or want, it is my privilege to provide." When he rubbed his hands over his hair, I noticed that they were trembling slightly. He was as emotionally on edge as I was. "I'm sorry. I'm sorry that I handled this all wrong, but it doesn't make my feelings, or anything we've shared less sincere."

I sighed and leaned back in the chair. "Well, then."

He stared at me. "What?"

I fought the smile that was blossoming inside of me. It was still terrifying. Committing to him wasn't just some light frivolity of the moment thing, not to me. It meant forever with him. I was beginning to see that my life with him in it could be great. *Our* lives, his, mine, and Nick and Casey's.

"What, Sky?"

I stood up and walked around his chair. "I didn't get a great sleep last night. I was thinking maybe we could take a nap." I waggled my eyebrows hoping he'd get the hint.

"A nap?" His voice sounded unamused, but he still stayed where he was, waiting for me to clarify.

"A nap." I put my hands on his shoulders and smiled down at him. "Aren't you feeling tired, Beast?" This time I winked and grinned seductively.

His eyes widened and he nodded. "Yes. Very."

I crooked my finger at him. "Come on, then."

He followed behind me, not touching me. "Are you saying what I think you're saying?"

I tossed a look at him over my shoulder. "Beast, you already signed our futures. You tied us together forever. I've just decided that, other than the fact that you didn't consult me first, you made a good choice."

∽

"*Fuuuck.*"

I stood in front of his bed and reached behind me to untie the dress straps at my neck. "You offering?"

Beast watched as my dress slid down my body, leaving me completely naked. "Tell me what you want, Sky."

I crawled onto his bed, slinking like a cat, my heart pounding. "I like when you take control here in the bedroom. When it comes to our sex life, I like my bossy, demanding Beast taking what he wants when he wants it. In *here.*"

He yanked his shirt over his head. "You're sure?"

I nodded. "I missed you."

He kicked off his pants and climbed on the bed with me. Wrapping his arms around me, he eased me down, hovering over me. "I missed you, my little mate, so fucking much."

"I'm still scared, Beast. I'm scared, but I'd be crazy to walk away from this. I feel what you feel." I put my hand over his heart. "I don't understand it, yet, but it's there."

"Love."

I buried my face in his chest and grinned. "Maybe."

He kissed the top of my head. "I'll take maybe."

There was more to be said, but it could wait. Beast kissed his way down my body and took his time feasting on me, making me come multiple times before he eased into me. Slow, easy, and steady, he rocked into me again and again until we both cried out our orgasms together. It felt perfect.

Beast held me in his arms as we both fought to regain our breath in the afterglow of our love making. "What do you think about marriage?"

I was still breathing hard, my heart pounding. "What?"

"Marriage. Cezar said it's a thing that humans do when they love each other."

I licked my suddenly dry lips. "Yeah, they do. Some of them."

"Good because I went out and bought our marriage certificate. I signed it and sent it in. I will give you a ring, but we are married, little one."

I sat straight up and my forehead bounced off of his chin as he sat up with me. "*What*?!"

He laughed. "Just kidding."

I slapped his chest and then shoved him. "You jerk! You scared the bejeezus out of me!"

He kissed me and pulled me closer against his body. "Is the idea of marriage to me so scary?"

I thought about it and shrugged lightly. "It wasn't the marriage. It was the control thing again."

He nodded. "So, if I asked, you would be okay with it?"

"Beast..."

He reached towards the bedside table and my heart stopped. "Sky, I want to spend forever with you."

His voice was solemn and serious and I clutched at my chest, my jaw dropping. What was happening? When Beast came back with a little bag of chocolates, one of which he popped into his mouth, I laughed out loud and slapped his chest again. "Stop it!"

He grinned and smeared a piece of the chocolate on my collar bone. "Eventually. When you are ready. We have time, little one. For now, I'm happy to just lick chocolate off you and live our lives like this."

"And the boys?"

"And the young males—*boys*." He licked the chocolate off and moaned. "You taste like heaven."

"What do you know about heaven, dragon?"

He met my eyes, his gaze burning into me with the intensity of dragon fire. "I know it intimately, mate. The taste, the feel, the sensation of you squeezing me as you come..."

I tilted my head back and moaned as he ran his tongue over the mark on my shoulder. "You are my heaven."

Maybe it was the mate bond—he'd said that we would each start to feel what the other felt—but in that moment I knew exactly what he meant. He, too, was the closest to heaven that I'd ever felt.

THE END.

NEXT BOOK IN THIS SERIES...

Small town librarian **Cherry Deschamps** *is perfectly content with her safe, mundane existence even if others might consider evenings spent with a mug of hot cocoa, bowl of Ramen noodles and a Netflix marathon boring.*

When the panty-meltingly gorgeous "Mr. Hollywood" enters her life, showering her with gifts and attention, of course she's skeptical. She's learned from an early age that exposing her heart will only lead to pain and heartache.

Cezar *fights every baser instinct he has to win over his human mate—including behaving in the ways of a human male. In the end, however, it may take the fiery passion and fierce possessiveness of his dragon to convince Cherry that she's worthy of being loved.*

P.O.L.A.R.

(**P**rivate **O**ps: **L**eague **A**rctic **R**escue) is a specialized, private operations task force—a maritime unit of polar bear shifters. Part of a world-wide, clandestine army comprised of the best of the best shifters, P.O.L.A.R.'s home base is Siberia...until the team pisses somebody off and gets re-assigned to Sunkissed Key, Florida and these arctic shifters suddenly find themselves surrounded by sun, sand, flip-flops and palm trees.

1. Rescue Bear
2. Hero Bear
3. Covert Bear
4. Tactical Bear
5. Royal Bear

∽

BEARS OF BURDEN

In the southwestern town of Burden, Texas, good ol' bears Hawthorne, Wyatt, Hutch, Sterling, and Sam, and Matt are livin' easy. Beer flows freely, and pretty women are abundant. The last thing the shifters of Burden are thinking about is finding a mate or settling down. But, fate has its own plan...

1. Thorn
2. Wyatt
3. Hutch
4. Sterling
5. Sam
6. Matt

∽

SHIFTERS OF HELL'S CORNER

In the late 1800's, on a homestead in New Mexico, a female shifter named Helen Cartwright, widowed under mysterious circumstances, knew there was power in the feminine bonds of sisterhood. She provided an oasis for those like herself, women who had been dealt the short end of the stick. Like magic, women have flocked to the tiny town of Helen's Corner ever since. Although, nowadays, some call the town by another name, ***Hell's Crazy Corner.***

1. Wolf Boss
2. Wolf Detective
3. Wolf Soldier
4. Bear Outlaw
5. Wolf Purebred

DRAGONS OF THE BAYOU

Something's lurking in the swamplands of the Deep South. Massive creatures exiled from their home. For each, his only salvation is to find his one true mate.

1. Fire Breathing Beast
2. Fire Breathing Cezar
3. Fire Breathing Blaise
4. Fire Breathing Remy
5. Fire Breathing Armand
6. Fire Breathing Ovide

RANCHER BEARS

When the patriarch of the Long family dies, he leaves a will that has each of his five son's scrambling to find a mate. Underneath it all, they find that family is what matters most.

1. Rancher Bear's Baby
2. Rancher Bear's Mail Order Mate
3. Rancher Bear's Surprise Package
4. Rancher Bear's Secret
5. Rancher Bear's Desire
6. Rancher Bears' Merry Christmas

Rancher Bears Complete Box Set

KODIAK ISLAND SHIFTERS

On Port Ursa in Kodiak Island Alaska, the Sterling brothers are kind of a big deal.
They own a nationwide chain of outfitter retail stores that they grew from their father's little backwoods camping supply shop.
The only thing missing from the hot bear shifters' lives are mates!
But, not for long...

1. Billionaire Bear's Bride (COLTON)
2. The Bear's Flamingo Bride (WYATT)
3. Military Bear's Mate (TUCKER)

Other books from Candace Ayers...

SHIFTERS OF DENVER

Nathan: Billionaire Bear- A matchmaker meets her match.
Byron: Heartbreaker Bear- A sexy heartbreaker with eyes for just one woman.
Xavier: Bad Bear - She's a good girl. He's a bad bear.

1. Nathan: Billionaire Bear
2. Byron: Heartbreaker Bear
3. Xavier: Bad Bear

Shifters of Denver Complete Box Set

Printed in Great Britain
by Amazon